PRAIRIE SKY

PRIMROSE SERIES
BOOK ONE

TANYA RENEE

To my Bear. I love you.

PROLOGUE

*E*ver stared into the stoic face of her father. They were at an impasse, neither willing to budge. Hot tears stung her eyes as she tried to keep her emotions and mounting anger in check. *Why was he being so unreasonable, so unyielding, so unsupportive?* she thought seeing his mouth harden in a straight line.

"No, Ever. I will not support you moving that far away." Hardin Wolton repeated as he glared into the face of his disbelieving daughter.

"This is what I want to do with my life. Can't you understand that? I cannot be a waitress forever. I cannot spend my life here balancing your books, just waiting for some guy to come rescue me from a mundane life!" she continued. "I want more for my future and this is the only thing I have been truly good at! And others think so too! It is hard to get accepted and they want me!"

"No." he repeated, slamming his hand down on his desk, making her acceptance letter fall to the floor. "And that is the last I want to hear about this!"

Ever glared back at her father, her face red with anger, still fighting back the tears that were threatening to escape. "Dad, you don't know me or even try to know me. You have never supported my dreams and now I have a chance to pursue them, and you shut me down!" she shouted, rising from her seat. "Maybe you love this farm. Maybe you are content to be here the rest of your life, but I want more for my life!"

"If you go, you are completely on your own!" he replied, his face twisted with irritation and frustration. "You will not get financial support from me."

Ever leaned over his desk, her tears now falling, and charged him with her brazen hazel eyes. Fury in their depths. "You think not giving me money is going to stop me?" she asked, unwavering.

"I hope you are prepared." He continued, a disparaging tone in his voice. "Its not easy out there in the world and you are not exactly a city girl."

Ever threw her hands up and started to pace her father's office, steam rising from her as she turned to face her father, closed her eyes, and took a long deep breath, trying to calm her frustration. "Daddy, I am not a little girl anymore", Ever whispered voice cracking with emotion.

"Ever…." he started, and she boldly held up her hand to him, halting his next comment.

"Daddy, I love you, but I'm going to do this with or without your support."

CHAPTER 1

The late April sky danced in hues of pink and purple with a hint of orange reflecting on what was left of the sun. Ever Wolton turned down the gravel road leading to her family farm. A large wooden sign coming into view with the words Prairie Sky Acres displayed in bold black letters. Worn and desperately needing a paint job, the silhouette of a horse, llama, and sheep still visible. She smiled a sad smile, thinking of her late father. Ever turned left and slowed to a stop, putting her vehicle into park, taking in the long driveway leading to the two-story farmhouse, cute and picturesque. A classic two-story home painted a cheerful yellow and trimmed in white with an inviting covered porch wrapping around the front of the house. The house, set a distance from the road, had a lush green front yard, was surrounded by wheat fields on either side and behind the house lay the farmyard and pastures. Prairie Sky looked like she remembered. Just as it looked in her rear-view mirror ten years ago when she left, swearing never to return.

Closing her eyes, memories of her childhood flooding back into her consciousness, she wiped away a stray tear trying to escape through her long lashes. Pulling out a compact mirror from her purse, she dabbed at her face with a tissue. Her face was flushed red and eyes sore and puffy. She had cried so many tears since her father's sudden passing two months ago. The long drive from Toronto to her Manitoba family farm gave her far too much time to think. Swallowing down hard, she drew in a deep breath and let it out slowly, trying to gain control of her emotions.

"You can do this," she whispered as she shifted into drive, making her way down the remainder of the long driveway leading to the house. Pulling her vehicle next to the house, she parked on the gravel parking pad. Exiting her car, she scanned the farm site across the yard. A large red hip roof barn stood like a beacon at the end of a path, surrounded by several paddocks and dense pasture beyond. The soft whinnies of horses and bleats of sheep echoed softly in the breeze. Ever gathered her long mahogany wavy hair around the side, closed her hazel eyes and breathed in deeply. The air was ripe with the smell of sweet hay, livestock, and lilacs. She smiled a nostalgic smile. *Smells like home.*

Shaking her head, she came around her car, putting her key in the trunk's lock. Suddenly, she was startled by a shrill, yet recognizable squeal.

"Ever!" the known voice shouted. Ever turned to see the familiar face of her childhood best friend Bea Baxter leaning over the side railing of the farmhouse porch, hand in the air waving vigorously.

"Hey there Bea! I was not expecting you to be here tonight!"

Disappearing, Bea's footfalls were heard bounding down the wooden steps, the walkway, then around the corner to Ever's car, stopping in front of her. Her wild curly red hair and bright green eyes beaming in welcome to her childhood friend. Bea's petite five-foot one inch frame, as always, making Ever feel large next to her pixie size friend. Despite her small stature, she made up for it with the size of her personality. Bold and sassy, she was as fiery as the hair on her head and a fiercely loyal friend. Wrapping her arms around Ever, she squeezed with surprising strength.

"I have missed you, Bea!"

"I have missed you too!" she replied, looking up at Ever, her emerald eyes twinkling with delight. "Welcome home!"

Ever and Bea released their embrace and turned to face the farmyard before them. The friends both stood there, taking a quiet moment to reflect. Bea turned her head to look up at Ever with sadness in her eyes.

"I am so sorry about your dad."

Ever met her sympathetic gaze and swallowed down the constricting lump building in her throat. Her dad was gone and now she was here to sort out his affairs. Here to deal with all the memories, both good and bad, then decide on the fate of the family farm. Her dad was a strong-willed man she both loved so much and resented all the same. A man she missed more with the realization that he was no longer here on this earth. The weight of the situation lay like a cinder block on Ever's chest. To avoid the tears threatening to escape again, Ever pushed down her emotions and turned back to her friend, giving her a resigned smile. "Thanks…" she replied with a deep sigh. "Never thought I would be here again."

Bea frowned and gave her another supportive squeeze, knowing how difficult this homecoming was for her friend. "Let's go inside and get you settled," she suggested.

Pivoting to face the car, Ever unlocked the trunk and Bea reached for a heavy suitcase, pulling it out with ease and starting up the path to the stairs leading to the porch and front door of the farmhouse. Ever shook her head in amusement and chuckled as she grabbed the remaining two duffle bags.

Meeting on the porch, Ever retrieved the key from its usual hiding place under the large ceramic flowerpot next to the door. Dusting it off, she put it into the lock and turned the key to her childhood home. Opening the door slowly, a rush of memories overtook her, memories she was not sure she was ready to relive.

With hesitation, her eyes roamed the narrow front entrance and staircase with the banister leading to the upstairs. A long hallway to the right led to the kitchen at the back of the house. A narrow wooden entrance table against the right wall held a brightly colored ceramic bowl she had made for her father during a middle school art class. A set of keys occupied the bowl, along with some loose change. Above it, the antique mirror she used to check her hair as she ran out the door to catch the school bus or meet her friends for whatever fun activity they had planned. Next to the entrance table was the sliding door to her father's office. Sliding the door open a foot, she peeked inside. A large, heavy oak desk was covered with stacks of papers, oak shelves filled with worn books and magazines, and a worn-out brown leather office chair. In the corner by the window, her father's old well-loved recliner and opposite from the recliner was a tall set of filing cabinets. She slid the door closed and resigned that soon she would have to go through his things.

To the left of the front entrance was a cased opening to the living room. The rustic stone fireplace with the oak mantel against the far wall displaying photos of family and friends and a large-framed sketch of her father with his prized show horse hung above it. A large brown leather couch angled to face the corner with an older model TV on a weathered wooden cabinet.

The house looked the same. A little dusty, but like nothing had moved or was out of its place. Just as it looked the day she left.

Ever ran her hand over the back of the leather couch, the softness of the leather inviting you to sit and stay awhile. She rounded the couch and stopped to look at the sketch above the hearth. She smiled, knowing how much her father loved that sketch and always said it was one of his prized possessions. Picking up a framed photo off the mantle, she grinned. She and her father were on horse-back after a trail ride. She was around 12 years old and loved nothing more than their time riding together. Her heart swelled at their happy faces in the picture. It was a simpler time, a time before animosity clouded their relationship. A time when she thought her dad hung the moon.

Suddenly, an overwhelming feeling of trespassing washed over her, and her father's harsh and hurtful words rang in her ear. *If you think this place is not good enough for you, leave! Go and don't even think of coming back!*

Ever could still feel the excruciating burn of his words and see the anger and disappointment on his face. Closing her eyes, she took in a deep breath, letting it escape in a long-pained exhale.

"Are you okay?" Bea asked, a look of concern on her face.

"Yes, sorry." she replied, shaking her head to wipe the memory from her forethought. "Just a lot of memories."

Bea gave her a knowing smile and silence filled the room as the pair stood there together in silent reflection. Breaking the silence, Bea asked, "How long do you plan to stay?"

Ever turned to her friend and replied, "My plan is until after the September long weekend. So just over four months." she answered. "Hopefully by then I will have made a decision about Prairie Sky."

"I know you will make the right decision." Bea reassured as the pair made their way back into the entrance and down the hall to the kitchen at the back of the house.

The retro kitchen was bright and spacious, with butcher block countertops and white wooden cabinets with black wrought iron handles. Against the far wall, a navy-blue vintage style gas stove stood with a copper hood vent overhead. To the right of the stove a copper double farmhouse sink, and a navy-blue vintage refrigerator. Lace curtains embroidered with cheerful daisies framed the large kitchen window over the sink and looked out over the farmyard. A large, weathered pine kitchen table with six chairs occupied the remaining open space. Ever smiled, taking in the welcoming country kitchen she had always loved so much.

"I have stocked the fridge, freezer, and cupboards, so you should have everything you need. I also made you a fresh pitcher of sun tea, just how you like it, with lemon and sugar." Bea explained, flashing her a sweet smile, then continued. "I have spoken to your father's farmhand who will meet with you tomorrow morning to go over the farm business and give you a lay of the land."

"Sounds good and thank you.", she nodded as a yawn escaped with her reply. Bea put her hand on her shoulder and gave it a gentle squeeze.

"You must be exhausted after all that driving. Let me leave you to settle in and get a good night's sleep. The bedding is fresh, and you should sleep well. I hope you don't mind the quiet city girl!" Bea joked with a sassy sideways smirk.

"I think I can handle it." Ever laughed tiredly. "Honestly, the quiet seems pretty great right now."

Ever and Bea made their way back to the front door. "Lunch tomorrow at the Eazy?" Bea asked, her eyebrow raised in question.

"Yes, sounds like a plan," Ever agreed, bringing her friend in for another hug.

With a bright smile, Bea embraced her, then moved into the hallway, opening the front door. Ever watched as she hopped down the porch steps to her bright blue Toyota truck, exclaiming. "See you tomorrow!"

Starting up her truck, Bea gave Ever a quick two finger wave as she rolled down the driveway towards the road.

Ever closed the door, and breathed deeply, the eerie silence of the house almost deafening. Turning, Ever entered the living room flicked on the lamps, making shadows cast on the walls. Surveying the room once more, she strode down the hall to the already brightly lit kitchen. Opening the fridge, she grabbed the pitcher of sun tea, took a tall glass from the narrow cupboard next to the fridge, exactly where she remembered them to be, and poured herself some tea. Taking a long sip, she savored the sweet and sour taste and sighed at the comfort it gave her. Looking around, she hugged the glass close to her chest and glanced at the kitchen table. So many meals and conversations had been shared there with her father. What she would not give to talk to him again or to hear his deep, bountiful laugh. Making her way back down the hall, she glanced briefly to the left at her father's office door. *Soon,* she thought as she opened the front door and stepped out onto the porch. The last of the sunset was fading into the horizon as she watched the stars brighten in the vast country sky.

Relishing in the quiet of the moment, she breathed in the crisp clean air and felt the chill of the late April night kiss her face. The wide-open space of the front yard was such a contrast from her home of the past ten years. She grinned in reflection, thinking of her quaint but bustling neighbourhood in the Lower East Side of Toronto. She loved where she lived. The incredible street art, interesting shops, galleries, trendy restaurants, and patios made it not only a fun place to live, but a great place to create and get inspired. She loved her studio apartment in a character home transformed into a six-plex apartment building. The large bright windows brought in natural light, perfect for her to paint by. A true artist's dream. It had been her dream for so long to live in the city and even with her farm girl upbringing; she fit into this stylish unique neighbourhood like a hand fits a leather glove. It was perfect for her. Despite a decade in the big city, Ever had to admit, the quiet of her family farm was a welcome reprieve and exactly what she might need right now.

"Perhaps getting out of the city will be good for you?" Her agent and friend Whitney had suggested. *"Perhaps this change in scenery and some fresh air will inspire you to create again."*

It had been three years since Ever's last gallery showing and it had been almost two years since Ever had picked up her paint brushes. At times, her fingers ached to hold them. Even then, no inspiration came. Thinking of this made an all-consuming fear of failure envelop her, and she sighed. Stepping down the stairs, Ever sat down on the top step, looking towards the expanse of night sky. The darkness had fully descended, and a million stars twinkled brilliantly above her. Memories of sitting here on this step with her father, looking at the stars as he pointed out constellations, enfolded her like a warm blanket.

She had missed this place so much. Sadness and regret consumed her. Despite the bitter last words, they spoke to each other that fateful day, Ever missed her dad more than words could express. Never had she thought she would never have spoken to him again. Never did she imagine he would be gone from this earth. Wiping away a single tear that rolled down her cheek, she swallowed down a sob threatening to escape. Gripping the glass of tea tightly to her chest, she stood, taking one more look at the beautiful stars shining above her. *To the moon and back, Daddy.* An excruciating tightness in her throat overtook her, she turned, going back up the stairs, onto the porch and through the front door, locking it behind her. The weight of loss, regret, and responsibility, heavy on her heart.

CHAPTER 2

The refreshing morning breeze rustled the curtains in Ever's childhood bedroom, bringing in the smell of sweet lilacs. Well rested, she sat up, yawned, and rubbed the sleep from her eyes. Swinging her long legs to the side of the bed, she stood up tall, arms above her head in a deep stretch. Glancing in the long mirror hanging from her closet door, she appraised herself. Ever had always been taller and curvier than most of her friends. This being a point of insecurity at times during her youth, she had long embraced her voluptuous body accepting her statuesque figure. Now at 30 it brought her confidence, as well as attention from the opposite sex.

Adjusting her sleep tank and shorts, she grabbed her terry robe, slipping it on, leaving it loose around her. Making her way out of the bedroom, she strode down the hall to the bathroom to take care of her morning needs, then down the staircase destined for the kitchen. The unmistakable smell of coffee enveloped her, and she breathed it in with appreciation.

Grabbing a mug from the cupboard, she filled it, leaving just enough room for a splash of milk, which she retrieved from the fridge. Steaming mug in hand she reached for the back door off the kitchen that led to the back deck. She put the hot mug gingerly to her lips as she looked out over the farmyard. Taking a sip of the warm amber liquid she closed her eyes, letting its soothing bitterness warm her throat.

"Hello." a deep rich voice sounded.

Startled, Ever jumped and looked around her quickly to be met by an unexpected stranger sitting in her father's rocking chair, holding a cup of coffee of his own. He had perfectly tousled light brown hair, a full groomed beard and mesmerizing ocean blue eyes that slowly crinkled on the sides. He looked rugged in a plaid, worn work jacket, faded blue jeans and dusty black work boots. Ever scanned him cautiously, only to be greeted with a warm, amused smile. His smile reassuring her, she let her shoulders sag as she breathed out and let out a nervous laugh.

Rising to greet her, he put out his hand in a friendly gesture. "Sorry to startle you, Ms. Wolton. The back door was open, so I made us some coffee. My apologies if I overstepped."

Ever surveyed him taking in his large frame that towered over her. His shoulders and chest were broad, his physique thick and muscular. His presence overpowering the space between them. Despite his intimidating size, he radiated a kind gentleness that both calmed and intrigued her.

Realizing she had not yet spoken, and the awkward silence was growing between them, she cleared her throat and shook her head to regain her wits. Putting out her hand to take his, she replied, "Please call me Ever. And you are?"

He took her hand quickly in a firm shake and apologized again, "So, sorry. Ben Hastings, your father's, umm, *your* farmhand." They both looked down at his huge hand holding her much smaller one. The contrast in size almost comical. She slowly looked up, meeting his intoxicating blue gaze, swallowed down hard, and gave him an amicable smile.

"Nice to meet you, Ben." she greeted, suddenly feeling self-conscious as she glanced down at her robe and pajamas. Noticing the tops of her breasts threatening to escape over the top of her sleep tank and long bare legs on full display in her very short pajama shorts, her face reddened.

Ben's eyes inadvertently grazed over her body and, realizing his stare lingered too long, he quickly looked away.

"Sorry." Ever laughed nervously and wrapped her robe over her curves and tied it to cover herself.

"It's okay, this is your home," Ben replied with a hint of a smile on his lips as he looked in the opposite direction. "I hope you don't mind that I made us some coffee. Your father and I would always enjoy a cup before we tackled the chores of the day."

Ever put her hands on her hips, cocked her hip to the side and looked up at him, her eyes twinkling in the morning sun. "Anytime you want to break in and make me coffee, you are welcome! Do you make breakfast too?" she teased, giving him a playful wink.

Ben, entertained by her lighthearted question, matched her. "Are you offering?" he asked with a baritone chuckle.

Ever grinned, taking in his question, bringing her hand to her chin as if giving it some thought. "Eggs and bacon?" she asked, eyebrows raised in question as she turned, opening the storm door to enter the kitchen. "Pretty sure I have all we need to make a hearty farm breakfast. Cannot work on an empty stomach after all."

BEN RAN his hand over his thick coarse beard and gave Ever a broad smile of agreement. Following her into the kitchen, he stole a moment to take in the curve of her body and rich reddish-brown hair, soft waves bouncing, still messed from sleep. She was more beautiful than he had remembered.

Having both attended Primrose High School, he was a senior when she was a freshman, making them almost four years apart in age. Normally their paths would seldom cross despite the small size of their high school, however every day he admired her from the back of the bus as she drifted on and took her seat. Tall and lanky in his teens, his height made him stand out, but because he was quiet and self admittedly nerdy, he never fit in with the popular crowd. From the moment Ever entered Primrose High School, she was the "it" girl. The girl all the boys wanted to date and was, without question, completely out of his league.

Through his final year of high school and after graduation Ben started working full-time at the local feed-mill so by the age of twenty the hard labour along with a final growth spurt not only helped Ben bulk up fully but also brought him to a towering six foot eight inches. Leaving Primrose at 21 for university, he lived in a dorm only coming home on weekends and would see Ever from time to time around town either with her dad or with her friends. Every time he did, he was awed at her natural beauty. And now, many years later, that undeniable beauty had only increased as she grew into a statuesque, stunning woman.

Ben stood back and waited as Ever rummaged around in the cupboards and fridge to retrieve the tools and food she needed to make them breakfast. "Can I help in any way?" he asked eagerly, rubbing his hands together.

"Sure!" she replied brightly. "How about you crack those eggs into that bowl and give them a scramble with that whisk?"

"That I can do!" Ben exclaimed, taking off his work jacket and rolling up the sleeves of his grey blue Henley shirt, taking a spot on the counter next to her. "How many do you want? I usually eat 4 or 5."

Ever unapologetically looked him up and down, making him feel very aware of her soft presence next to him. She offered him a cheeky grin and replied. "I have no doubt you do."

Ben smirked, giving her a sideways glance.

"Two eggs are fine for me, big guy!" she joked, as she lit the burner and added the bacon to the cast-iron skillet.

Ben was never so thankful for his full facial scruff as he was now, feeling a warm blush creep up his cheeks from her flirtatious teasing.

As Ever finished their breakfast, Ben seated himself at the kitchen table, taking in the graceful way she moved around the kitchen. *Dear Lord, she is gorgeous.* Realizing he was staring, and his mouth had dried, he took a long sip of his coffee as Ever plated their breakfasts. Turning around, Ever presented him with a big plate of fluffy eggs and bacon.

Taking his plate, he offered her an appreciative smile. "Thank you, this looks amazing!"

Ever touched his forearm and gave him an appreciative smile. Her fingertips lingering briefly but memorably on his warm skin. It was such a small gesture, but the effect of her touch made his body instantly aware of her. "While we eat, can you give me a run-down of what we are doing today?" she asked, taking a seat next to him.

He nodded and shifted, giving her more room and could not help but enjoy her proximity to him and how their arms brushed as they both dug into their breakfasts. As they ate, they talked lightly about the general morning chores, what needed to be done today, and the menagerie of animals currently residing on the farm.

Ever picked up a slice of perfectly cooked bacon. Taking a bite, she closed her eyes and let out a low moan of appreciation.

Ben's head turned to her, his blue eyes widened, and

he swallowed down slowly, feeling the guttural sound deep in his core.

She opened her eyes and met his, her cheeks taking on a rosy hue. "Bacon is my aphrodisiac." She laughed nervously.

Almost choking on his coffee, he cleared his throat and returned his gaze to her. "Noted." Ben replied deadpan, the corners of his mouth slowly lifting in a grin.

Both Ben and Ever burst out in a fit of laughter as they returned to their breakfast and conversation. Draining their mugs, they both stood from the table, taking their dishes to the sink.

"I'll do these later." Ever declared, reaching out to take his plate. As she grabbed his plate her hand covered his. Both slowly met each other's eyes. Something intangible passed between them in that moment. An intense spark of attraction making goosebumps instantly rise on his arms. Noticing her shiver and her breath hitch, he could see Ever felt it too.

Not wavering his gaze, he took the plates from her. "You cooked so I will clean."

"Thank you." Ever replied, stepping away from him as if processing what had just happened. "Mind if I quickly get dressed and join you back down here in about ten minutes?"

"Go ahead. I will be here waiting," he answered, flashing her his handsome smile as he put the dishes in the farmhouse sink.

Her head spinning and her face flushing with heat, she quickly turned, rushing out of the kitchen, and up the stairs to get ready for the day ahead.

* * *

EVER QUICKLY CLOSED her bedroom door, resting her back against it, breathing heavily, her face hot and her body even hotter. *What the hell was that?*

Never had she felt such an immediate attraction to a man. Something so palpable it made her head feel light and her vision blur. When she touched his hand, the bolt that went through them was unquestionably electric. *What am I doing?* Ever closed her eyes to gather her thoughts and inhaled a shaky breath. "Ben is my farmhand." She whispered softly to herself, trying to stop the flutter of butterflies in her belly. "He is here to work for me," she went on, trying to remind herself of this fact. "I can't get involved." Softening her shoulders, she sighed. *But he is so sexy,* she mused, biting her bottom lip. *I am in so much trouble.*

Taking a deep steading breath, she quickly removed her pajamas then slipped on a pair of worn boyfriend jeans and a grey form fitted long sleeve t-shirt. Grabbing her hairbrush, she brushed out her long locks and fashioned them into a messy ponytail. Slipping into the hallway, she made her way to the bathroom to freshen up, brush her teeth, and smoothed on some moisturizer. She looked up into the bathroom mirror and smiled, happy with what she saw. She never had been a glamour girl. Never felt the need to spend her commissions on fancy makeup. Moisturizer, ChapStick and when going out a touch of mascara was all she needed. Low maintenance and natural. Exactly the way she liked it.

Letting out another nervous exhale, she descended the stairs and made her way into the kitchen, where Ben was putting away the last of the dishes, a towel draped over his broad shoulder. *Damn, how does he make that look so good?* Turning her way, he caught sight of her and inadvertently looked her up and down, his eyes flashing with approval.

Ben met her eyes as a faint blush appeared on his cheeks. Clearing his throat, he glanced away to disguise his obvious appraisal.

Was he blushing? She grinned at the realization that she was affecting him as much as he was affecting her. And if she was being honest with herself, she liked it. She liked it a lot.

Slipping on a pair of her father's work boots, sitting by the back door and large work jacket, Ever laughed, realizing how ridiculous she looked swimming in her father's clothes.

"Why don't we go to the farm supply store later today and get you boots and a jacket that fit?" Ben suggested with a laugh, taking her in.

Ever nodded as she opened the storm door and trudged her way across the deck to the stairs and down to the gravel path leading to the barn, Ben following. They strode side by side across the yard toward the big red hip roof barn.

"Big Red!" she exclaimed.

Ben smiled and slid the rolling barn door open, revealing a long aisleway flagged by 12 box stalls, six on each side. The tall ceiling and wood rafters made a nice contrast from the metal of the box stall gates. At the back of the barn was a feed room, tack room and barn office. As they walked down the barn aisle, a little tabby barn kitten scampered past them, and Ben reached down to scoop it up. Ever smiled, taking in this giant of a man as he held the little kitten in his huge hands, petting it gently. Something about this huge man holding something so vulnerable and tiny made her chest warm. He met her eyes with a melting gaze and put the kitten into her hands. It purred, looking up at her with its sweet face and meowed. They both smiled and Ever set it down gently, letting it scamper away.

They continued down the aisle towards the barn office and Ben unlocked the door. Piles of papers and file folders were neatly organized on the desk. The walls were covered with brightly colored ribbons, and the built-in shelves along the far wall were full of trophies from her father's horse showing days. Having spent most of her childhood weekends at horse shows with her father, she appreciated the work that went into acquiring those accolades. Her father was well known for his cowboy prowess, and she enjoyed watching her father ride and compete.

Ben followed her perusal of the room in appreciation and offered Ever a smile. "Your father was an impressive man."

Taking a seat across from the desk, a constrictive lump of sadness formed in her throat. She breathed in raggedly and whispered. "Yes, he was."

Ben met her eyes, sensing her sorrow and reflected her sadness now on full display. "I am so sorry for your loss."

Ever looked down at her hands, trying to steady

herself, and let out a long-pained exhale. Meeting his sympathetic gaze, she asked, "Did he ever talk about me?" her voice breaking with the question.

"All the time." Ben nodded, looking into her anguished eyes. She smiled back, a look of regret on her face as a rogue tear escaped, making its way down her cheek.

Ben got up and rounded the small desk, stopping next to her and crouching down beside her chair. He reached over and tenderly brushed the single tear from her cheek with his calloused thumb, making her instantly feel comforted. She met his eyes again, so full of compassion and she offered him an appreciative smile.

"I think I just needed to hear that. We had not talked for so long. Somehow, I wondered if he forgot about me," she confessed, letting out a sigh.

Ben shook his head and smiled kindly. "Hardin was a man of few words and although he never said much, I could tell he had a lot of regrets."

Ever searched his eyes at his reassuring comment and gave him a sad smile. "Thank you."

Ben rose to his feet and put his hand out to Ever. "Ready to feed the animals?" he asked.

Ever looked up at this gentle giant of a man feeling a sense of comfort enrobe her, making her feel protected and safe. She took his offered hand and rose to her feet as they exited the office together.

TOGETHER THEY FED and watered the sheep, goats, llamas, and horses. As they worked, they lightheartedly shared stories about her father, their families and people they mutually knew from town.

"You mentioned you live in the city now. What city do you call home?" Ben asked with curiosity as he leaned on the gate, resting his arms on the top rung.

"Toronto. I moved there about ten years ago." She replied, patting one sheep on the head.

Ben gave her a warm smile as he picked up the hose to fill up the water troughs. "What brought you there?"

"Art School. I loved it so much there, I decided to stay," she replied thoughtfully.

"Loved?" Ben questioned.

"Yeah." she hesitated. "I mean, I still love Toronto but lately I haven't felt very inspired there."

His eyebrows raised in question, and he stopped what he was doing, giving her his full attention.

"I am an artist. A painter actually and my last gallery showing was three years ago. It has been a while since I have painted. I hope a change in scenery will help."

Ben nodded, acknowledging her reasoning and Ever continued. "With my dad passing and having to figure out what to do with his estate, I figured now was as good a time as any to come back. Not sure what I am going to do yet."

Ben glanced her way, taking a moment to process her admission, then spoke. "Obviously I love Prairie Sky and my job here, but don't let me sway your choice," he offered. "I will be fine with whatever you decide."

"What are you going to do if I decide to sell Prairie Sky?"

Ben leaned against the gate, crossing his legs, formulating his answer to her question. "Well, I have a Bachelor of Arts in Agriculture and Business." Ben replied. "So, I have a few options. The dream is to own a farm one day, though."

"So, this farm hand thing isn't just a job for you?" she asked with a playful wink.

"Not at all." Ben laughed. "After I graduated, I worked for a few businesses, including my family hardware store, which my brother now manages; Hastings Hardware."

Ever nodded, knowing the store he was referring to.

"Your father was looking for help both with the farm work and with managing the business end. So, he hired me. That was seven years ago now. I live just down the way, about four miles west of here."

"So, you are a Primrose High Graduate?" Ever inquired, eyebrows raised as she locked the paddock gate.

Ben flashed her a huge smile. "I am. Class of 2007. I was a senior when you were a freshman."

Ever looked up at him suddenly meeting his gaze with an amused smile curling up her lips. Ben caught her inquiring look and gave her a resigned smirk with a shrug.

"Did you know who I was back then?" Ever asked, putting her hands on her hips and jutting one hip out to the side.

Damn, she is gorgeous. Offering her a smile, he paused, knowing there was no way to deny it, and met her inquiring gaze. "I did. You were hard to forget," he admitted.

"You liked what you saw?" she continued playfully volleying it back at him.

Ben looked away quickly as he felt his cheeks warm. *How does she do that to me?*

"You know you are cute when you blush." she laughed as she picked up the feed bucket, put her hand on his muscular bicep and gave it a squeeze. "Glad I was memorable," she continued coquettishly as strode into the barn.

Ben's breath caught with her touch, his heart pounding in his chest as his eyes followed the sway of her hips as she walked away. The effect she was having on him was hard to describe. The attraction between them was palpable. Her presence made him both nervous and excited. *A little too excited*, he thought. *How am I going to resist her?* He asked himself as he turned to follow her.

* * *

THEY FINISHED up the morning chores and, after updating Ever on the current farm business, they made their way back to the farmhouse.

"So, what's on the agenda for you the rest of the day?" Ben inquired, glancing at his watch.

"Going into town to meet Bea for lunch at the Eazy. And you?"

"I'm heading into town too." Ben answered. "I need supplies for some paddock repairs this afternoon."

"A farmer's work is never done!" Ever exclaimed as she turned around to face Ben, a whimsical look on her face.

"It never is," he replied, giving her a sweet smile. "Meet later this afternoon at farm supply?"

"It's a date!" she offered, flashing him a dazzling smile with a wink.

With flushed cheeks, he took in her words, and his lips curved into a smile. "See you later."

"Wouldn't miss it!" she shouted, knowing exactly what she was doing to him.

CHAPTER 3

*P*rimrose was a typical prairie town, 40 minutes southeast of Winnipeg and 20 minutes from the small city of St. Augustine. With a population of just over 2000 residents, it was a quiet close-knit community surrounded by family farms and vast open fields mainly comprising wheat, canola, and sunflowers. The town had two schools, one church, a post office, a mechanic shop, hardware store, an insurance agency, a firehouse, a feed mill in the centre and exactly two places to grab a meal, Lings Chinese Food restaurant and the coffee shop/gas station/anything your heart desires store called "Eazy Café and Gas Bar."

Ever pulled up to the Eazy and got out of her car. The sign on the front was wooden and worn, the same sign that graced the front of the building when she was a kid. She smiled at the fond memories of this place. A place she hung out at with friends and worked at in her teen years. It had not changed and was still the best place to get a greasy burger, as well as the latest piece of town gossip with your visit.

Ever stepped into the cafe and was greeted with the smell of fried onions and burgers on the grill, as well as familiar and unfamiliar stares from the patrons occupying the tables and booths. Their curious stares were followed by whispers as Ever spotted Bea sitting in their favorite booth along the back wall.

Bea jumped out of the booth and slow motion ran to Ever, wrapping her arms around her when she reached her.

"You always know how to make me laugh!" Ever exclaimed, throwing her head back in laughter.

Bea shrugged and flashed her a sassy smirk as she made her way back to their table. Ever took a seat across from her and picked up her menu.

"What's good here?" Ever asked cheekily as she paged through the ancient menu.

"Ha! That menu has not changed in the last twenty years!" Bea laughed. "Same greasy goodness! Want to share a Cheeseburger platter like the old days? Oh, and two chocolate shakes?" she asked, raising her eyebrows in question.

Slamming down the worn, cracked menu on the table, Ever replied. "Deal!"

A bubbly blonde teen waitress took their order, and they settled into their booth with familiar ease.

"So, how was your first morning back at the old homestead?" Bea asked with curiosity, taking a sip of her water.

"Kind of surreal. Feels strange but good to be back as well." she replied. "Did the morning chores with Ben, got acquainted with the animals, and he walked me through the current farm business details."

"So, you met Ben?" Bea asked, a glint of mischief in her question.

"I did." Ever smiled in reflection. "He surprised me this morning. I must have left the kitchen door open, and he made us coffee. We had breakfast together before heading into the barn. Do you know him well?"

"Girl, I know everyone!" she answered with a big guffaw, then continued. "Ben is a great guy, literally one of the best. He lives with his younger brother Hayden in their childhood home, not far from you. Both his parents passed away in a car accident a few years ago. His parents ran the local hardware store and since their passing Hayden runs the family business. Ben helps him from time to time, but his heart is on the farm. He is a farm boy through and through."

Ever nodded in agreement. "Yes, you can tell he loves it. He said he hoped to have his own farm one day."

"Yeah, that man was destined for farming. Built for it too! He is huge!" Bea exclaimed, throwing her hands up to emphasize her point. "Like a freakin' tree!"

They both giggled like two schoolgirls chattering over a boy.

"They definitely broke the mold when they made him." Ever agreed with an appreciative smirk. "He sure is handsome, too. If you are into that huge, muscly, rugged country boy look..." she trailed off, staring beyond her friend in thought, her teeth gripping the corner of her bottom lip.

Bea leaned back on the bench and crossed her arms,

her lips curving up in a knowing smile. "You like him already, don't you?"

Ever focussed back on her friend, a huge smile on her face, knowing Bea could read her like a book. "He is so sweet. He has this quiet gentleness about him that seems like such a contrast to his size. It's kind of intriguing," she replied, and let out a little whistle. "And he sure is pretty to look at."

Both Ever and Bea looked at each other, then broke into a fit of giggles as the door chime sounded.

"Speak of the devil…" Bea whispered from the corner of her mouth, her eyes darting towards the door.

Turning, Ever looked up and to see Ben, his imposing frame taking over the café entrance. His bright blue eyes surveyed the tables and stopped when he spotted them. His right hand went up for a casual wave and he flashed them a blindingly handsome smile. Ever's gaze was locked in admiration for the man acknowledging them from across the room.

Bea looked at Ever in amusement with a huge, wicked grin.

Ever caught her look in her peripheral vision and whispered. "I am so screwed".

"With any luck…" Bea winked at her friend coyly.

Ever choked out a laugh as Ben slowly strode to the back, fielding greetings from locals and stopping at their table.

"Hey Big Ben!" Bea exclaimed playfully.

Ben turned to Bea and smiled to match her amusement. "Hey there, Bitty Bea!"

Bea let out a bountiful laugh as Ben's gaze settled on

Ever. She nervously licked her lips at the intensity of Ben's focus on her. His eyes darted to her moistened lips as silence settled over the trio. Awkwardly, Ever cleared her throat and shifted in her seat to face him. "Hi!" she blurted out quickly. "Long time no see!"

Ben laughed, and his eyes crinkled endearingly at the corners. *How I want to reach up and touch those beautiful lines. Perhaps run my fingers through that beard?* Ever shook her head to remove the distracting thoughts.

"Want to join us, Benny?" Bea asked as she gestured to the open spot next to Ever, giving her a sly wink.

"Sorry no, I wish I could. Just picking up some take-out. You ladies have fun, and I will see you perhaps at 4 p.m. at the Farm Supply?" he confirmed, bringing his attention back to Ever.

She nodded, flashed him an agreeable smile, and kicked Bea under the table as she was still smirking at them both.

He gave Ever another heart-stopping grin, acknowledged them both brightly, turned and moved towards the cash register. Paying for his food, he grabbed his takeout bag and turned around to give them one last smoldering glance before he exited the café.

Bea returned her attention to Ever, pure enjoyment radiating on her face. "Holy crap! Is it hot in here?" she asked a little too loudly.

Ever rolled her eyes and shook her head, a hot blush creeping up her face. *Hot indeed!* she agreed to herself as she watched him go.

** * **

BEN DEPARTED the Cafe and hopped into his truck, tossing his lunch next to him on the passenger seat. Firing up the engine, he gripped his steering wheel, stealing a deep breath before shifting the truck into drive and pulling out of the gravel parking lot. As he eased down the main street of Primrose, his thoughts drifted to Ever. Her mesmerizing hazel eyes with flecks of gold that twinkled when she smiled. Her creamy skin and the long curve of her neck when she put her hair back that he so wanted to reach out and touch. His fingers tingled at the thought and a deep yearning formed in his chest. The way she laughed with him and shared so openly with him. How she was so vulnerable with him in the barn office this morning. Making him ache to hold her in his arms and stroke her back softly to console her. *Had I ever felt the overwhelming desire to care for and protect a woman? Was the attraction and need as overwhelming for her as it was for me? No question.* He could see it in her eyes. She was as drawn to him as he was to her.

At 34, he had done his share of dating. A few made it past the first few dates, but he had never had a serious relationship. He was not a saint, having had his share of casual physical experiences, but he had never felt such an intense and immediate connection with anyone until now and he was not quite sure what to do about it.

* * *

OVER THE NEXT TWO WEEKS, Ben and Ever settled into the easy routine. Early mornings, sharing coffee and breakfast together, followed by chores and errands together in town. Their ease of laughter, lighthearted conversation, and flirtatious banter made each day go by quickly.

Ever enjoyed his deep baritone laugh as they joked and his sly glances towards her when he thought she was not looking. His gorgeous blue eyes made her melt with even the smallest of looks. She had it bad, and she knew it. She was crushing on him more than she wanted to admit, considering their employer/employee dynamic and if she was being honest with herself, she wasn't even feeling guilty about it.

Every night, his presence crept into her dreams. Hot, steamy dreams. His eyes were dark with lust and his come-hither grin consumed her, making her ache to touch him. How she longed to run her hands through his sexy, disheveled hair, down his deliciously handsome face and over his muscular shoulders, chest, and stomach. *Get yourself together,* she scolded herself every night, only to fall asleep again, overtaken with racy dreams of Ben Hastings and all that she wanted to do with him.

BEN TOSSED and turned and finally opened his eyes to stare into the darkness. He swung his legs out of his bed and held his head in his hands. Ever was consuming his every thought, and he could not shake the deep longing he felt for her. The constant ache for her, making him sleep deprived. He had not slept well over the past two weeks since Ever arrived at Prairie Sky. Every time he closed his eyes, she was there, beautiful, wanton before him. *Get a grip,* he chided himself. *She is your employer.*

When he accepted the job from Hardin Wolton, he of course knew who Ever was. He knew how incredibly beautiful she was, but now getting to know her and spending so much time alone with her, his schoolboy crush was morphing into full-blown desire. A desire he was finding difficult to ward off.

Letting out a deep exhale, he rose from the bed and made his way down the long hallway, through the living room, and into the kitchen.

Opening the fridge, he took out the milk, and he turned on the stove burner. *Perhaps some warm milk would help me sleep.* As he pulled out a sauce pot and poured a generous amount of the creamy liquid into the pan, he heard the familiar jingle of keys and the front door lock disengage.

Hayden must be home. He thought, looking up to see the old wooden clock turn to midnight. "Hey there Cinderella!" he exclaimed, as his younger brother joined him in the kitchen.

"What are you doing up at this hour?" Hayden asked as he ran his hand through his short, medium brown hair. "Warm milk? Breaking out the big guns tonight?"

Ben smiled resoundingly and glanced at his younger brother. Standing six feet tall, Hayden was much smaller in stature than his brother was. Where Ben was broad and thick, Hayden was leaner and more toned. Although they obviously did not look exactly alike, they shared the same ocean blue eyes and handsome smile. He leaned against the island, arms folded, giving Ben a questioning look.

"Been having a hard time sleeping lately." Ben exhaled out with exasperation.

Hayden nodded his head, a knowing grin slowly creeping up his face. Cocking his head to the side, he considered his brother for a moment. "Could this disruption in sleep have anything to do with the lovely Ms. Wolton? She sure is gorgeous!"

Ben looked up at his brother and gave him a searing look squinting his eyes.

"Just calling it like I see it, bro!" Hayden exclaimed, holding his hands up in the air.

Ben swallowed dryly and returned his attention to the milk boiling on the stove. Turning off the burner, he poured the milk into a large mug and took a seat at the island.

Hayden took a seat next to him and pivoted to survey his big brother, continuing his interrogation. "She's got you all bent out of shape, hasn't she?" Hayden asked pointedly with an amused smirk.

Ben looked up from his mug then took a long sip of the creamy warm milk, feeling it soothe him. Resigned, he nodded in answer.

Hayden leaned back and crossed his arms over his chest. "Are you going to ask her out?" he asked.

Ben looked up at Hayden quickly, meeting his brother's eyes, and let out a huge guffaw. "I can't! She's technically my boss."

Hayden followed his answer with a chuckle. "And..." he trailed off.

"What if I do and it doesn't go well? What if we get serious and break up?" he questioned.

Hayden gave his brother a broad smile, stood from his stool and patted him on the shoulder. "What if it works out?" He asked, playing devil's advocate. "I would ask her, Ben. If you don't, I am sure someone else will." Hayden added, exiting the kitchen.

Ben stared into his mug in contemplation. *Would she say yes? Would things get awkward?* So many questions and scenarios were running through his head all at once. If he were to be bold and take a risk in pursuing Ever Wolton, without question, she would be worth it.

CHAPTER 4

*E*ver turned down the gravel road leading to Prairie Sky. The unmistakable orange of her father's Kubota tractor came into view, with Ben at the wheel. Ever's jaw dropped, taking in the scene. Ben aloft the tractor, shirtless in all his tantalizing sweaty muscled glory. His tanned skin glowing in the warm May sunshine, a light smattering of hair above his perfectly formed pecs, and a thick cinched waist. *Was that a 6 pack?*

Ever could feel the drool pooling at the corner of her mouth and she bit her bottom lip in appreciation. "Dear God, give me strength." She muttered out loud to herself as she parked her car.

Exiting the car, naughty thoughts of Ben burned in her brain. Ever retrieved several bags of groceries and carried them into the house. As she put down her bags on the kitchen table, she heard the loud rumble of the tractor and glanced out the kitchen window to see Ben parking it beside the barn. Ever shook her head and blew out a breath slowly. *How can one man be so incredibly sexy?* She asked herself. Shaking her head, letting out a giggle at her inappropriate thoughts, she went back out the front door, hopped down the porch stairs, and made her way back to her open trunk to get the rest of her groceries. Spotting movement in her peripheral vision, she turned to see Ben leaning against the house, watching her with a friendly smile, still in all his shirtless splendor, work pants sitting low on his hips, the delicious V of his hips on full display. Ever nervously took a deep breath and exhaled quickly to steady her pounding heart. She turned to him and asked huskily, "Done for the day?"

"I am," he replied as he drifted over to meet her. "Do you need help bringing in your groceries?"

"I think I can handle the last of the groceries, but I could use your help with carrying in the box and easel." She replied, gesturing to the backseat of her car. "It's a little heavy for me."

Ben opened the back door and grabbed the large box with ease, holding it with his left arm and grabbing the easel with his right, his amazing muscles flexing.

Ever looked on in awe and let out a little nervous laugh. "I had a hard time just getting that into the car! Should have brought the muscle with me to town today, I see!"

Grabbing the last of the groceries, she swayed past him, giving him a teasing wink, climbed the porch stairs and entered the house, with Ben following closely behind.

"Where do you want this?"

"Just put that box down in the corner by the living

room window and can you set up the easel in front of the picture window?" she asked as she made her way to the kitchen to deposit the rest of the groceries on the kitchen table.

Rejoining Ben in the living room, she watched as he positioned the easel in front of the large window overlooking the front lawn.

"What is all this stuff?" he asked, gesturing to the large box he'd carried in.

Ever strode over, crouched down and opened the box to show him the paint, palettes and brushes she ordered.

His eyes brightened, giving her an approving smile. "Are you preparing to paint?"

"I am.", she replied. "Or hoping to, I think would be more accurate", she said, looking down at the box and over to the easel.

Ben pursed his lips together and gave her a slight frown, acknowledging her struggle. "What type of painting do you do?" he asked with genuine interest, wanting to brighten her mood. "Not that I know that much about art."

Ever smiled up at him, loving his thoughtful question. "Impressionism mostly. Have you heard of Claude Monet?"

"Water Lilies." he offered proudly.

"Yes!" she exclaimed in surprise. "You know more than you think you do," she appraised him, making him grin.

"So, what has inspired your work in the past?" his questioning continued.

"Oh, goodness, so many things! Most of my past work

would come from strolling through my neighbourhood in Toronto and a park not far from my apartment. Trinity Bellwood's Park. Have you heard of it?"

"I haven't. Tell me about it," he insisted with curiosity, leaning back against the leather couch.

Ever pivoted herself to take a seat on the hardwood floor and stretched her long legs in front of her, leaning back, resting her weight on her palms. "It's this urban park in the middle of a trendy neighbourhood in Toronto. Sort of an urban oasis, but still very busy with cyclists, runners and the like. It has the most gorgeous view of the CN Tower between the trees; lots of flowers. Bustling, yet peaceful, too. Like the best of both worlds. It's one of my favorite places in the city." Ever mused thoughtfully.

Ben smiled, his kindness radiating through, as he took in her description. "Sounds nice. Perhaps I should visit sometime."

She mirrored his smile, meeting his persistent gaze. "I would love that."

Companionable silence fell between them, until Ben cleared his throat, breaking their silence. "I should go. Hayden is dragging me out tonight. Beers and babes!" he declared with a roll of his eyes. "Hayden's words, not mine," Ben corrected, a flush on his cheeks.

"Oh, the life of single, hot country boys!" she teased with a giggle as she bent her legs to stand.

"Let me help you up," he offered, extending his hand to her.

She looked up at him, meeting his kind gaze, and accepted his hand. "Thank you."

Ben pulled her to her feet, underestimating his strength, and she crashed into his bare and hard as concrete body. Putting both hands up instinctively to brace herself, she looked down, only to realize both of her hands were resting on his very hard, very impressive pecs. She couldn't help but splay her hands over the hard muscles as they reflexively twitched under her touch. His hands were now on her waist to steady her. Her T-shirt lifted slightly, exposing a thin band of skin. As if involuntarily, his hand caressed the bare skin, making her breath hitch at the sensation of his touch. She bit her bottom lip, inhaling the heady smell of fresh cut grass, sweat and musky male, making all her senses go into overdrive. Darting her tongue out to wet her lips, Ever looked up to meet his blue eyes, intense and hungry, making her core instinctively pulse. She swallowed slowly, looking again towards his impressive chest under her palms, then nervously back to his eyes flashing him a playful grin. "Lay off the weights, big guy, you got bigger boobs than I do!"

Ben's eyes slowly crinkled at the corners, and he let out a deep, bountiful laugh. Ever, her cheeks flushed, laughed too as she removed her hands from his chest and stepped back from his strong hold. Shrugging, Ever offered him another smile and swayed past him towards the door, her head still spinning from their closeness. "Thanks for your help and have fun tonight!"

"What are you doing tonight?" he asked, trying to be nonchalant with his questioning. "Are you and Bea going out to paint the town?"

"Paint the town? How old are you, Mr. Hastings? I

believe my generation calls it whooping it up," she dead-panned with a twinkle in her eye.

"Oh, pardon me, Ms. Wolton! Will you be out, whooping it up?" he asked with a volleying laugh.

"Perhaps!" she shrugged in reply. "Will we run into you men folk carousing about town?"

Ben laughed again, appreciating the way she made him laugh. "Perhaps." He responded, giving her a wink as he made his way down the porch stairs towards his truck.

BEN STRODE towards his truck and glanced back at the stunning beauty lingering on the porch, needing to take her in again. He turned away and shook his head, looking down at his hands, still tingling from touching the soft skin at her waist. His face warmed as he remembered how she felt close to him. The sweet smell of her skin, like vanilla ice cream. So close he could see the flecks of gold in her hazel eyes. Those eyes so full of nervous wonder and desire. *Yes, that was desire*, he thought. In that fleeting moment, he felt her want for him, too. An acknowledging smile overtook him as he rounded his truck, opening the driver's side door. "Yes." he whispered to himself with determination. "I'm going to ask her out."

EVER OPENED the front door to find her friend's bright and beautiful face. Bea's emerald, green eyes were framed with lush long lashes and her lips were glossed with the most luxurious shade of red. Her fiery red hair was worn down with her signature wild curls. She wore a black razor back tank top, tight black jeans and killer brown suede cowboy boots meant to do some serious dancing and, if need be, serious ass kicking. She looked like a little country goddess.

"Holy smoke, Bea! You look incredible!" Ever exclaimed, gesturing for her to spin around.

Bea slowly turned around, giving her friend the full view, and bowed. "I try." she winked slyly.

Bea stopped and appraised her friend. Ever wore a white loose fitting off the shoulder peasant blouse, dark wash skinny jeans and black low heel ankle boots. She wore her hair loose in waves and had her naturally beautiful face made up with mascara and lip gloss.

"You look gorgeous! Urban but country too! I love it!" she commented with appreciation. "These dirty old country boys will not know what hit them!"

Ever beamed down at her tenacious friend. *Oh, how I've missed her.* After Ever had left Primrose, they had kept in touch, but Bea was only able to visit her a handful of times. When she did though, her life of the party presence always made Ever feel happy. They created many fun memories, touring Toronto's hot spots and sipping cocktails on the patios of King Street. Bea could fit in no matter where she was, and Ever admired that.

Grabbing her house keys and a small crossbody bag, they made their way out onto the lit-up porch, and she turned to lock the door. "So where are we headed, BB?" she asked playfully.

Bea rolled her eyes at the nickname Ben gave her and

flashed a mischievous smile at Ever. "The Pickled Pig over in St. Augustine! It's this old-time honky-tonk bar, totally cheesy, super fun atmosphere! Great drink specials, fantastic music, and an awesome dance floor! Also, the crowd is mixed so us oldies won't look like cougars! "

"Cougars? We are barely 30!" Ever choked out in laughter.

"Yep, cougar status has been activated! We want to go where the real men are!" Bea replied with a wink as she got into her truck.

Ever followed her into the passenger seat and turned to question her. "Which men, may I ask, will be there?"

Bea's lips lifted into an amused grin, knowing exactly what her friend wanted to hear. "Last I heard, Hayden, BEN…" Bea emphasized enunciating his name.

Ever settled into her seat and buckled her seatbelt. *Ben would be there*, she thought. A feeling of nervous anticipation settled in her stomach as she reflected on their encounter that afternoon. There was no one else she wanted to see more.

Bea pulled into the parking lot of "The Pickled Pig", a winking bright neon pig perched on the front wearing a cowboy hat greeted them along with music and laughter wafting from the bar filling the parking lot.

"This place looks like fun!" Ever smiled brightly, clapping her hands with excitement.

Bea nodded with a smile and eagerly bounded out of the truck. Ever followed suit and rounded the vehicle to meet her. "Let the fun begin!" Bea exclaimed, looping her arm through Ever's.

Both women giggled like teenagers as they entered the

bar, the familiar sound of Luke Bryan's "Shake it for Me" blasting through the speakers. Surveying the crowd, it did not take long for them to spot the guys leaning against the long bar. Ben's height, broad shoulders, and shaggy brown hair stood out like a beacon calling them over.

As they approached, Hayden turned, spotting them, and shouted above the loud music. "Ladies!" then whistled in appreciation, taking them both in. Ben turned and met Ever's eyes. His eyes gleamed as he drank her in brazenly, making her face flush with heat at the intensity of his perusal.

"Hey BB!" Ben acknowledged her friend as she gave him an affectionate shove. Ben gave her a quick wistful smile and brought his attention back to Ever locking her in with his persistent stare.

Hayden looked over at Bea and his eyes widened.

Bea smiled back, mouthing; "I know, right?" and shrugged.

Hayden glanced back and forth from Ben to Ever. "Are you going to officially introduce me, Big Bro?" he asked, clearing his throat to get his attention.

Breaking their connection, Ben offered his brother a smile. "Hayden, this is Ever Wolton. Ever, this is my brother, Hayden Hastings."

Ever put out her hand to shake and Hayden flashed her his debonair smile. Taking her hand, he put it to his lips, kissed it and flirtatiously gave her a wink. "Pleasure to meet you, Ever!"

Bea rolled her eyes and gave him an exasperated punch in the arm.

Ben growled under his breath.

Startled, Ever's eyes darted to Ben, and an amused smile curved her lips. "Did you just growl?" she asked with a giggle.

His eyes met hers and softened in answer.

How cute! Like a big bear. She mused to herself.

Hayden's eyes twinkled with delight as he looked back at his brother. Ben flashed him a dirty "back away and you won't get hurt" look. Shrugging, Hayden laughed, knowing he was getting under his brother's skin. "What can I get you ladies?" Hayden offered as he turned to the bartender. "This round is on me."

"Surprise us!" Bea shouted playfully as she looped her arm in Hayden's and turned to give Ever a mischievous wink.

As Hayden and Bea waited to order drinks from the bartender, Ever took a moment to take in her surroundings. The bar was dimly lit, with raised booths surrounding the perimeter. The extra-long oak bar top was flanked by a mirrored backdrop and three long wooden shelves of alcohol bottles. Bright neon signs graced the walls in fun designs and sayings, with a huge wooden dance floor in the middle. Even by Toronto standards, this place was unquestionably cool.

Ever returned her attention to the giant of a man next to her, giving him a coy smile of approval as her eyes examined him with appreciation. "You clean up nice cowboy!"

He wore a light blue button-up shirt, the top three buttons open, showing off his impressive physique. Thigh hugging dark wash, boot cut jeans and brown cowboy boots finished off his look. In one word he looked–

yummy. Ever smiled at her thought, inadvertently biting her bottom lip, then glanced up at him flirtatiously through her lashes, meeting his unwavering gaze.

BEN'S MIND was reeling as he watched Ever bite her bottom lip, the action going straight to his groin. *What would he give to run his tongue over that lip? Nip it. Suck on it.* Wicked thoughts overtook him, making him very aware of his body. *What would it be like to kiss her?* The feeling of anticipation was as thick and heavy on him as it obviously was on her. His breath laboured as he took her in again. She was a knockout. Her silky mahogany hair flowed in natural waves, her flawless skin, long lush lashes framed her intriguing hazel eyes. Her mouth-watering curves strategically accented by her flowy off the shoulder blouse and tight dark wash jeans. Ben had never seen a woman look sexier.

Hayden and Bea returned, disrupting his naughty thoughts with drinks in hand. Beers for them and two cocktails for the ladies. "Long Island Iced Tea!" Bea presented to her friend with a flourish.

"Yum!" Ever exclaimed, taking a long pull from her straw, closing her eyes, and letting out a satisfied moan.

Ben's eyes hooded instantly as he took in her guttural sound. His body responded instinctively in appreciation.

Ever opened her eyes and looked up to meet his hungry gaze. Her face flushing, she commented huskily, "Sorry, it just tastes so good!"

Hayden and Bea simply watched Ben and Ever with

interest and amusement as if waiting for something to happen between them, resulting in an awkward silence between the foursome. Ending their observation, Bea slapped Hayden on the back and suggested. "Why don't we go say hi to a few friends and leave these two alone?"

Hayden, taking her hint, wiggled his eyebrows and followed Bea, disappearing into the crowd.

Ben gave his brother a sideways smirk, took a long pull of his beer and rocked on his heels, nervously letting his eyes drift over the crowd.

Ever admired him thoughtfully, head cocked to the side. "Do you dance?" she asked.

"I can... yes," he responded. "Do you want to dance?" he asked, putting his beer down on the bar and reaching for Ever's drink. She nodded, took another long sip from her straw, and quickly handed it to him. "Do you know how to two-step?"

"No, but can you teach me?" she asked, bouncing with excitement.

"I would love to!" Ben replied, flashing her a confident smile. Taking her hand and leading her to the middle of the dance floor, he looked down at their feet and showed her the movement with his own. "Slow, slow, quick, quick. Make sense?" he asked, raising his eyebrows in question. "Don't worry, I'll start us off, and you just follow my lead."

Ever nodded with delight.

Ben started to move, and she quickly picked up on the tempo, following him step for step, gliding across the floor. She beamed with joy and a giggle escaped her lips when he whirled her around, turning her to go another direction. Ben relished the feel of her close to him. Her soft hand in his and his large hand splayed on her shoulder blade. His fingertips instinctively reached for the bare skin, brushing it lightly. She radiated in his arms, laughing and squealing with each twirl and spin. Pure joy marked her beautiful face and his heart swelled at her happiness.

After a few up-tempo songs, the music transitioned to a slow song, "Amazed" by Lonestar. Both still laughing and breathing hard, Ben still holding her hand. He raised his eyebrow in question. Ever nodded, no words needing to pass between them, just knowing that they wanted to continue to dance with each other. Ben wrapped his strong arm around her waist and pulled her into him, his right hand still holding hers. A faint gasp escaped her throat as he brought her flush with his body, looking up at him nervously but with approval. He took in the feel of her so supple against the hard concrete of his body. Such a contrast, like cotton against steel. Looking down into her stunning eyes, a deep longing formed in his chest and with the hitch of her breath, he knew she was feeling it too.

EVER SMILED up at his unbelievably handsome face and was overcome by a feeling of warmth and desire building low in her core. The butterflies in her stomach fluttered strongly as he held her close and swayed to the gentle beat. The movement of his rock-hard body against hers made her feel lightheaded and needy for him. He brought their coupled hands in close to their bodies, an affectionate gesture aligning their hearts. As she looked down at their fingers intertwined so perfectly, she felt all her resolve melt away. She could no longer fight off her attraction to him. Her heart hammered in her chest, and she could feel his pulse, fast and steady, against the back of her hand. Her rapid breaths synching with his. Deep with desire and sparking with electricity, she looked up at him and licked her lips to steady herself, knowing exactly what he wanted, because she wanted it too. The burning heat of his hunger seared her with a single question. *Yes*, she nodded, wanting nothing more than his lips to touch hers. Slowly Ben leaned down, never wavering his gaze from hers. Stopping mere millimetres from her lips, they stole a final breath together, hot and heady with anticipation. Her eyes fluttering closed, she felt his deliciously soft lips cover hers, igniting a flame in her heart.

✳ ✳ ✳

BEN COULD FEEL the desire burn from deep inside her as his lips gently, wantonly moved over hers. He felt her give into him fully, all doubt gone as she melted in his arms. His tongue darted out boldly, tracing the rim of her lips until they parted, allowing him in, his tongue sliding with hers in a beautiful tangle. He deepened their kiss, feeling the passion in him rise, wanting to consume her in every way. She tasted so sweet, like a ripe red strawberry in the summer. Pure perfection. Like no other kiss he had experienced before or would ever again. Their searing kiss lit a match inside his chest, burning a trail straight to his heart.

Ben knew, right there on that dance floor, that there was no other woman he would want to hold, kiss, and someday soon, make love to. Ever Wolton was his. They parted breathlessly and with a single look into her rapturous eyes, he knew she had claimed him too.

CHAPTER 5

They danced the night away, laughing till their sides hurt and stealing kisses as much as they could. Kissing him felt natural to her, like they were always meant to kiss. She could feel the sexual tension building between them with each tender touch of his fingers on her skin when they danced. It was intoxicating and made her head spin. She felt drunk on the feelings he was stirring in her, and she could not get enough. Inevitably, the night had to end, so she pulled Bea aside. "Do you mind if Ben gives me a ride home?"

Bea grinned naughtily, giving her a little waggle of her eyebrows. "Go climb that tree!"

Ever burst out laughing and shook her head at her friend's crazy comment. "Will you be okay to drive Hayden home? Pretty sure he will need a ride".

"Yep, I am way under my limit so I can take that goon home." She replied, looking at Hayden putting the moves on a busty brunette on the dance floor. Bea shook her head. "That boy has no pride."

They both laughed and Bea conceded, flashing her a wicked grin. "Go on, get out of here, have fun and don't do anything I wouldn't do!"

"So, anything I want!" she quipped back to her friend with a giggle.

"Pretty much!" Bea laughed, giving her a shrug.

Ever turned and sauntered back to Ben, slipping her hand into his.

"Are you ready to go?" he asked, giving her one of his devastatingly handsome smiles.

"Yes!" she replied.

They waved to Bea and Hayden and to a few other people they knew as they left the bar, hand in hand. Getting to Ben's truck, he led her to the passenger side and opened her door for her. The chivalrous gesture not lost on her, she went on her tiptoes and kissed him chastely on the lips. Giving her a tender smile, he helped her into the truck. He circled back to the driver's side and hopped into the cab, his hands gripping the wheel as he turned to meet Ever's intense gaze. *I want him so much*, she thought, transfixed by his beautiful eyes, so full of passion and promise. Feeling her body vibrate with a nervous desire, she slid up next to him, wanting to feel his closeness and warmth. Wrapping his large arm around her, he pulled her into his chest and started tracing his fingertips under the edge of her blouse, over the exposed skin of her shoulder. The heat of his touch making goosebumps cover her skin. Resting her hand on the taut, hard muscles of his stomach, her hand burned from the heat radiating off him. Ben shivered from her touch, and she smiled up at him wantonly, loving that he was feeling the intensity of the building tension between them, too.

"I like touching you." She whispered, peering up at him through her long lashes, licking her lips and letting her fingertips slip boldly between the buttons of his shirt to his bare skin. He groaned and quivered under her touch.

"God help me Ever; I'm having a very hard time being a gentleman here," he confessed, his lustful eyes darting to her. Resigned, she flashed him a playful smile and patted his stomach, then slid back to her side, buckling her seat belt. Turning to him, she gave him a satisfied smirk.

He let out a deep growl, making her laugh in amusement.

"Bring me home, you Big Bear."

Ben let out a long exhale, conceding to her sweet term of endearment for him with a smile as he fired up the truck and pulled out of the parking lot.

Ever reached for his hand as they drove back to Prairie Sky, a contented quiet falling on them both. She relished the feel of a large, warm hand in hers as his thumb stroked hers affectionately.

Parking next to the farmhouse, Ben exited first and came around to open her door. Swinging her legs out to jump down from the cab, he caught her by the waist and lifted her down slowly, her body sliding down the hard length of him, making her breath hitch. An unmistakable look of hunger on his face, he closed her door and engulfed her in his strong arms, holding onto her earnestly. She could feel his rapid heartbeat against her cheek, making her own increase in time with his. They stayed there, enrapt in each other's arms, feeling the deep connection they could no longer and would no longer fight. Releasing her from his hold, he smiled and tenderly took her hand in his, leading her down the gravel walkway to the farmhouse. Together, hand in hand, they climbed the porch stairs to the front door. Standing at the door, he looked down at her with deep adoration in his eyes. Running his hands through her hair, his fingertips caressing the nape of her neck, making her shiver under his touch. Bringing his other hand to her face, he caressed her cheek and ran his thumb over her bottom lip. His gaze intense and hazy with desire, he leaned down, brushing his lips softly to hers.

Feeling intoxicated by his sweet kiss, she moved to run her hands through his hair and deepen their connection, pulling him into her. Her desire igniting, their tongues met like a match being lit, smoldering passion bursting into a flame. He tightened his grip on her body, claiming her mouth as his, all his self-control leaving him. Lifting her to his waist, her long legs wrapped around him as he pressed her back against the solid wood of the front door, their kiss spiraling into a full-blown fire. His lips left hers, roaming to her earlobe, giving it a tender nip, making her whimper with need. Kissing down her neck, he blazed a trail with his tongue over her collarbone, making Ever moan in appreciation. Her throaty sounds made him growl in reply.

"You're going to kill me, Ever." he whispered huskily, completely breathless. Putting his forehead to hers, he panted out his breaths, as he tried to regain control. "If we go inside right now, I know all my self-control will be gone."

"Maybe I want you to," she confessed, her face flushed with a sexy, kissed senseless glow.

He growled deeply at her words as he captured her mouth in another scorching embrace. He pressed her body harder into the door. The hardness and heat of his body against hers sent her mind reeling.

"I need to stop, Ever." he groaned out, breaking their kiss again, this time letting her slide down his body and setting her gently to her feet. She gave him a slightly dejected look, and he shook his head to reassure her, his eyes meeting hers with sincerity. "I want to spend the night with you. Ever, there is nothing I want more right now, but I want it to be special when I do, so I need to ask you something."

Still breathing heavily, her lips red and swollen from their intense make-out session, she looked up at him in question.

"Will you go out on a date with me?" he asked, his face flushed and his voice coming out ragged.

She stared at him a moment, but blinked and took in his question. "Don't you think we have passed that already?" she asked with a smile tugging on her lips.

"Seriously, Ever, I want to take you out. Let me romance you before we pick up where we have left off tonight."

Ever searched his hopeful eyes, realizing he was completely serious. Stretching her arms around his neck, she ran her fingers through his disheveled hair and down his face through his soft beard, loving the feel between her fingers. "Yes, I will go out with you, Bear." she whispered in answer, her eyes twinkling in the dim porch light.

Taking her face in both of his large hands, Ben leaned down for one last excruciatingly gentle kiss, making her knees wobbly and weak. Releasing her, he stepped back, descended the porch steps, and stole one more glance at the radiant woman leaning over the porch railing, illuminated in the moonlight.

"Goodnight, Bear." she beamed as she blew him a kiss.

Pretending to catch it and put it in his shirt pocket, he replied. "Goodnight sweetheart".

EVER OPENED HER EYES, a warm smile curving her lips. She reached up and touched them, feeling them tingle at the memory of Ben's kisses. So soft and gentle at first and then so deliciously hard and demanding. *Damn, that man can kiss*, she thought, getting lost in the vision of his wanton dark eyes boring into her and the scorching heat radiating off him. Her core pulsated at the thought and her pulse quickened in anticipation of seeing him today.

Glancing quickly at her phone, she saw a text from Ben pop up on her screen. *"Good morning, sweetheart. Coffee? See you downstairs."*

Ever grinned and held the phone to her chest, relishing in his endearment for her. *Sweetheart*, such a simple thing to call someone, but coming from Ben, it felt so special, making her heart flutter.

Quickly she dressed, putting on a worn Tragically Hip concert t-shirt, a faded pair of boot cut jeans with rips on her knees and brushing her wavy locks into a messy bun at the top of her head. Speedily taking care of her morning needs, she hurried down the stairs eagerly making her way to the kitchen. As his text promised, there was Ben, leaning against the counter sipping his coffee and looking like every woman's sexy farmer fantasy. A weathered baseball cap on his head, a navy body-hugging t-shirt was stretched over his broad muscular chest, and brown work pants sat low on his hips. He approached her, handing her a steaming mug, then leaned down to brush his lips to hers, making her melt into a puddle right there on the kitchen floor.

"Good morning," she greeted, her face flushing from the syrupy sweetness of his embrace.

"Good morning," he replied, his smiling eyes crinkling at the sides like she adored. "How did you sleep?"

"So good," she sighed, biting her bottom lip. His eyes instinctively darted to the lip she held with her teeth and his eyes darkened. Reaching for her mouth, he ran his thumb over the lip, freeing it, and leaned down to kiss her again. Releasing their kiss, she wrapped her arms around him and sighed, making them both smile.

"I picked up breakfast from the Eazy. Fresh Cinnamon Buns." he offered, gesturing to the bakery box on the kitchen table.

Brightening, she released him and clapped her hands together. "Yes!" she exclaimed, turning her attention to the table, and lifting the bakery box lid, to be met by the most heavenly smell of butter, brown sugar, and cinnamon. Retrieving one, she bit into it and moaned in satisfaction. Cream cheese icing graced her top lip.

Ben let out a little chuckle and shook his head, then wrapped his large arms around her back, cradling her in his warmth. "Your sounds are so crazy sexy!"

Ever turned her head to the side to catch his gaze with a twinkle of mischief in her eyes. "How sexy?"

He growled, his soft scruff tickling her face, making her shiver as his tongue darted out to lick the icing lingering on her top lip. Ever giggled and turned in his arms to face him. With her cinnamon bun still in hand, she scooped icing into her finger, smeared it on his lips, then reached up to take it off in a sticky sweet passionate kiss, making a growl rumble from his throat.

Breathless, she broke their embrace, and she wiped the remaining icing from his lips, then sucked it off her finger, giving him a flirtatious look.

"Ever.", he scolded, his voice deep and growly. "As much as I could kiss you all day, we need to get the chores done. Besides Ms. Wolton, I promised you a date tonight."

She appraised him with an excited and curious look on her face. "Where are we going?" she asked.

"You'll find out," he answered with a twinkle in his eye.

"Well, what do I wear?" she asked, putting her hands up on the air in question. "A girl needs to know these things."

He reached out and cupped her cheek, caressing it gently, making her soften to his touch. "Sweetheart, wear whatever you want. You are always the most beautiful woman in the room."

She met his blue gaze with a glint of mischief in her eyes. "If you keep complimenting me like that, you may just get lucky tonight!" she winked.

Ben laughed, his deep voice croaking slightly as his face heated with a blush. Ever reached up and planted a chaste kiss on his lips and gestured him to follow her. "Let's get these chores done and then you can romance me, cowboy."

* * *

"WHAT HAPPENED LAST NIGHT?" Bea asked curiously as she browsed through a rack of blouses at a boutique in St. Augustine. She picked one off the rack and held it up herself in the store mirror, analyzed her reflection, then put it back on the rack.

"A lot of kissing." Ever answered simply as she perused a rack of dresses.

"I could see that!" Bea laughed. "You two were like a moth to a flame last night. I was wondering if you were going to undress each other right there on the dance floor. It was kind of intense!"

Ever's face heated as she flashed back to their passionate encounter on the porch. "Intense is accurate." She agreed, giving her friend a wink. "Seriously Bea, I don't think I have ever been so attracted to a man before. I feel this powerful pull towards him. Butterflies, fireworks, the whole nine yards." Ever shook her head and laughed as she continued to comb the rack in front of her. "Seriously, listen to me going on and on about him. I am 30, for goodness sake!"

Bea surveyed Ever taking in her excitement. "But have you ever been in love?" she asked pointedly.

"Honestly, no," she replied, shaking her head. "I mean, I

have dated my share but never anything super serious or very long term. No one has ever interested me that much."

Bea acknowledged her words and replied. "But with Ben?"

Ever paused and looked up, thinking about her question. Reflecting on Ben's handsome smile and mesmerizing blue eyes, she thought about how he made her feel. He made her feel so beautiful and seen. Truly seen. Like he knew exactly who she was, faults and all, and still wanted her. Around him she felt protected, like he would never do anything to break her heart or hurt her. "With Ben, I could see it getting serious." She replied simply. "He makes me feel safe, and I am not sure anyone, but my dad made me feel that way. Before our fall out, of course." She added with a frown.

"That's saying a lot!" Bea exclaimed. "Ben reminds me of your dad in many ways. A strong, quiet type. He is almost kind to a fault and honestly, I think he would do anything to protect the people he loves. Seriously, Ever, Ben is one of the good ones."

Ever smiled, liking Bea's comments.

"After the past couple of months, you've had, you deserve some happiness." Bea declared as she continued her search of the racks. Suddenly, Bea squealed and held up a dress to show Ever. "This is it! It so you, Ever! It's simply perfect!"

Ever took the hanger from her friend, holding the dress up to her body in the mirror, and smiled in approval. "It really is!" she agreed, her face beaming with delight.

"Ben is going to flip his lid when he sees you tonight!"

CHAPTER 6

*B*en walked up to the front door of the Prairie Sky farmhouse with a large bouquet of daisies in hand. His heart was pounding in his chest and his palms felt sweaty at the thought of spending the night romancing Ever. He chided himself with a chuckle. *Get yourself together, man.* Taking a deep breath, he knocked on the door and it flew open. Ever greeting him with her gorgeous smile, his eyes widened, and his jaw dropped to the floor as he took her in. She was stunning. Ever stood before him in a cheerful yellow dress that hugged her curves in all the right ways. The cap sleeves showed off her toned arms and the sweetheart neckline skimmed the tops of her breasts. Cinched at the waist, the beautiful dress flared out to just below the knee, making it look flirty and a little retro. Delicate daisies embroidered on the neckline and hem made the dress as unique as the woman wearing it. Strappy high heel sandals finished her outfit. Her hair was pulled back in a twist, with mahogany waves kissing the sides of her face and neck. Her face glowed naturally with simple, glossed lips. She looked like a dream. He tried to speak, but the words wouldn't come out.

Pleased, and a little amused by his reaction, she asked. "Do you like it?" as she twirled around, making the skirt lift playfully above her knees.

"Yes, yes, I do." He stammered, his voice coming out deep and raspy.

Handing her the bouquet of daisies, her eyes danced with delight as she accepted them. "Thank you. Daisies are my favorite."

He smiled and cleared his throat, trying to tamp down his nervousness.

"Just give me a minute while I put these into some water."

Ben waited in the front entrance patiently as she scurried off into the kitchen. Taking a deep, cleansing breath, he watched her disappear down the hallway. *Damn that dress*, he said to himself as he let out a long exhale. Although he knew the taste of her sweet lips, the feel of her soft skin under his fingers and how her body molded into his so perfectly, tonight he felt like that awkward nerdy kid in high school who admired her from the back of the bus. *Seriously, get your head on straight*, he scolded himself. Ever Wolton was literally his dream girl, and now he was about to go on his first date with her, and if last night was any indication, he would spend the night. Returning, Ever immediately wrapped her arms around his neck, flashing him her gorgeous smile.

"Hi."

"Hi" he replied, meeting her smile, feeling his

awkward nervousness subside with her affection. "You look absolutely breathtaking," he whispered as he leaned down to brush his lips to hers.

She smiled into his kiss and pulled back, asking. "So, where are you taking me, Bear? I am literally starving!" her stomach growled at that moment, echoing her words.

Instinctively, Ben put his large hand on her belly, and she scorched him with a heated gaze. Feeling bold, he smiled down on her, a coy smile curving his lips. "I'm starving too."

* * *

PULLING up to a brightly colored restaurant on the outskirts of St. Augustine, Ever looked up at the sign. The sign read, "The Blue Corn."

"Is this a Mexican restaurant?" she asked excitedly.

Ben flashed her a confirming smile.

She bounced in her seat and squealed with delight. "I am totally obsessed with Mexican Food."

With a look of pride and satisfaction at her reaction, he opened her door in full gentleman mode and hand in hand they entered the restaurant. They were greeted with brightly painted walls and intricate handmade papel picado hanging from the ceiling in bold colors. The restaurant was loud and boisterous, full of patrons laughing and enjoying their meals. The most delicious aromas filled the air, making Ever's mouth water. The savory smell of fresh homemade tortillas, spicy slow cooked meats and chilis filled her senses. It was heavenly. Ever felt her stomach rumble again and Ben turned to her having heard her stomach over the noise of the restaurant. His eyes crinkled in amusement, and he pulled her close to him, giving her a kiss on the head affectionately. "I promise this will be worth the wait."

A beautiful older woman with long silver hair pulled back with a clip, greeted them. "Hola, Ben! It is nice to see you again!" she welcomed them with her thick Mexican accent, her kind eyes dancing with delight. "I see you have brought a lovely lady with you!"

"Nice to see you as well, Mrs. Perez." Ben greeted in return. "Yes, this is my.... Ever."

Ever looked up at him. *She was his Ever.* She liked that.

Mrs. Perez took Ever's offered hand in greeting and held it for a moment, offering her a gracious smile. "Please call me Rosa. It is so nice to see a beautiful woman with handsome Ben here." She commented, giving Ever's hand a squeeze and Ben a wink.

"It is so nice to meet you, Rosa." Ever offered, immediately liking her. "You have an amazing restaurant here."

"Oh, gracias!" she thanked as she grabbed two menus. "I have a special table for you two lovebirds."

They followed her through the large restaurant to a booth in the back corner that was tucked away from most of the other patrons. Adorned with a bright Mexican tablecloth and lit by a soft glowing lantern, the booth was cozy and intimate. Sliding into the booth next to each other, Rosa smiled at them sweetly and handed them their menus.

"The Pork Carnita Tacos are on special tonight with a side of Spanish rice and beans. I will be right back for your drink orders and with some complimentary chips and salsa."

"That sounds wonderful! Thank-you." Ever replied, smiling at the sweet woman as she happily hurried off to greet more incoming guests.

Ever looked around, taking in the colorful and inviting interior, then met Ben's waiting gaze. "Wow, Ben, this place is amazing!" she exclaimed cheerfully, taking it all in. "I don't think you could have picked a better place!"

"I thought you might like it." Ben smiled proudly, knowing he had picked the perfect place for their first date.

Rosa returned with a basket of warm chips and fresh homemade salsa, taking their drink and food orders. Both opted for the special, along with a cerveza for him and a lime margarita for her.

As they waited for their food, Ever gave Ben a curious look, tilting her head slightly to the side. "You intrigue me, Mr. Hastings." she mused. "Why is a handsome, hardworking, ambitious man like yourself still single?"

"At my age?" he continued.

"Yes! I mean, you must have women throw themselves at you all the time!" she teased, taking a sip of her margarita.

He laughed, his deep baritone reverberating within the confines of their booth. "No." he answered. "I mean I have dated, but no one really interested me enough to commit."

"No serious relationships?" she questioned.

He shook his head in answer. "And you?" he asked, his eyes transfixed on her.

"Never had one." She answered honestly with a shrug. "I have dated, but have never had a boyfriend."

"Not even in high school?" he asked, his eyebrows raised in question. "You were probably the most popular girl at Primrose High."

She laughed and reached out for his hand, stroking it affectionately. "Being popular does not always translate into dates."

Silence fell between the pair and Ben met her gaze, his eyes so soft and sincere, then deadpanned. "You were just waiting for me, weren't you?"

Ever laughed and squeezed his hand, and he winked at her as he took a sip from his cerveza.

"What were you like in high school?" she asked, genuinely curious as she popped a chip into her mouth.

Ben leaned back against the booth and gave her an "are you sure you want to know" look.

"C'mon, you seem to have known everything about me back then! I want to know what you were like!" she urged, giving his forearm a squeeze.

"Well, I was super tall, awkward, not very athletic, although I did play basketball because of my height. Very studious, I usually got good grades. My head was usually in a book. Kind of a loner. I spent more time watching Star Wars movies than socializing with others. It would be safe to say I was a nerd."

Ever grinned at his description and flashed him a coy smirk. "I like Star Wars and nerds."

Ben laughed and slid his hand around the nape of her neck, brought her in close and captured her lips in a mind-bending kiss. Releasing his embrace, she reached up to touch his soft lips with her fingertips and cupped his face, making him close his eyes and lean into her touch. *Have I ever seen a more handsome man? Have I ever felt so wildly attached to someone?* "Ben, I like you. I like you a lot," she confessed, sliding her fingers through his beard eliciting a low deep guttural growl from his throat. *Oh, how I love that growl.*

Ben opened his eyes and beamed at her, his eyes crinkling with happiness. "I like you a lot too," he replied and brushed another tender kiss to her lips then pulled her into a big bear hug.

Was she ready for this? She silently questioned. *Would she be able to go back to Toronto in the fall if she started a relationship with this man? Would she be able to say goodbye to him?* Looking into his hopeful eyes tonight, all she wanted was to throw out all her apprehensions and jump in feet first, not knowing how she would land.

* * *

THE FOOD and drinks were amazing. They talked, laughed, touched, and stole kisses as they enjoyed their meals together, basking in each other's company. Their seemingly endless conversation and flirtatious banter made him high on Ever. She made him laugh till his sides hurt and was so unapologetically authentic that he found himself hanging on every word she said. He could not stop touching her, kissing her, just marveling at her presence here with him. He felt like the luckiest man on earth.

Realizing how much time had gone by, they left the restaurant, satisfied and full. He helped her into the truck and climbed in himself, stealing a glance at Ever. "What would you like to do now?" he asked, gripping the steering wheel, the sexual tension from the night before thick in the air.

She flashed him a coquettish grin and raised an eyebrow. "Do you need to ask?"

He took in her words, knowing exactly where their night was going, and glanced at her, meeting her expectant gaze. "Are you sure? We could go out on some more dates and…"

She leaned across the seat and slid her index finger over his lips to silence him. "I want you."

A low growl escaped his throat, and she smiled, pulling her seatbelt over her, buckling herself in. "Take me home, Bear."

He did not have to be told twice. Rushing out of the parking lot, he made his way to the highway leading to the farm. They didn't talk, the building intensity between them growing by the minute. Ben's groin was tightening in anticipation, and he prayed he would stay on the road. Periodically she would flash him a sexy grin, knowing exactly what she was doing to him.

They pulled into Prairie Sky in record time and Ever turned to Ben, letting out a giggle. "Eager?" she teased.

His lips curled up in a smile and not replying, he unbuckled himself and leaned over to unbuckle Ever. Swooping her up, he settled her on his lap, making her gasp in surprise. Meeting his hooded gaze, she tenderly touched his face and ran her fingernails through his beard as she shifted to straddle him, causing the skirt of her dress to lift, exposing her upper thighs. Taking his face in her hands, she crashed her lips to his as they kissed passionately, tongues moving together like a dance. She ground her hips over his hardness, making him groan in her mouth as his hands ran up the backs of her thighs to cup her behind. She broke their embrace, letting out a moan of approval against his mouth.

"Let's go inside," he growled out breathless and wanton. She nodded, and he opened his door, setting her down first and then sliding out after her. Taking her hand at first, then impatiently swooping her into his arms.

"Bear!" she exclaimed with a giggle at his impatience as she held on to him tightly.

He laughed at her reaction, his voice deep and raspy. Reaching the door, she fumbled with the lock, still in his arms. Once inside, he set her down gently. She turned around, pinning him with her hungry gaze. Dropping her purse to the floor, she slowly slipped off her sweater, tossing it next to her purse and leaned down to unfasten her sandals, eyes never leaving his. Fixed in her stare, he turned the lock to the front door. The heat between them mounting by the second. She backed up toward the stairs, playfully gestured him to come closer with the crook of her finger and flashed him a come-hither look. *Fuck, she is sexy*; he appraised his heart pounding against his chest. Complying with her request, he stalked over to her but before he could reach her, she turned and bolted up the stairs, her giggle trailing after her.

He followed her, searching the darkened rooms, finding her at the end of the hallway, in what must be her bedroom. She stood facing him, bathed in moonlight, then reached up to release the comb holding her hair. Her beautiful reddish-brown waves cascaded down past her shoulders, and his breath caught, taking in her beauty. *Radiant.* He reached for her pulling her closer and their lips met in a scorching kiss, hot and heady. Running his hands boldly over the curves of her body, as she groaned in appreciation. Nipping her bottom lip, he released it and blazed a trail of kisses down her neck, across her collarbone and over the tops of her breasts, causing goosebumps to form on her skin.

"Help me out of this dress.", she demanded breathlessly.

Turning her around, he slowly lowered the zipper, making her tremble under the touch of his fingers on her back. Fully unzipped, he slid the dress over her arms, letting it drop to the floor in a pool at her feet. He leaned down and kissed her shoulders, making her shiver from his lips on her heated skin. Her supple skin, like silk under his lips. Her scent, a mix of vanilla and sweet Ever, doing inexplicable things to his body, his lust for her like a dam ready to break.

Slowly, she turned around to face him and he drank her body in. Wearing a light blue demi-cup bra which barely contained her ample breasts and matching bikini panty, only a miniscule strip of lace covering her most intimate part. His mouth watered to taste her. Her waist was soft but trim and her hips an enviable hourglass. Her skin was flawless and incandescent in the moonlight. He had never seen a more beautiful body, and he wanted to explore every inch.

* * *

EVER'S CORE pulsed with need as Ben admired her with lust and appreciation in his eyes. She reached to him and started unbuttoning his shirt, hands quivering with desire. Sliding his shirt down over his large strong shoulders and arms, her fingertips explored the hard angles of his upper body. The taut skin, like steel under her touch. *He is so beautiful*, she marveled. All hot tanned skin. Her fingers continued their exploration running over the ridges of his stomach tracing the line of hair disappearing into his jeans. Trying to steady her breath, she reached for his belt buckle and undid it slowly, looking up at him through her long lashes. He met her with a look of pure need melting any lingering resolve she had left. She dragged the belt away and released the button on his jeans. Feeling his hard length pushing at the front of his jeans, she slowly unzipped him, letting her fingers tease the waistband slowly and deliberately. He groaned and took over, slowly moving his jeans over his hips and down his muscular thighs to reveal his black boxer briefs. She smiled in appreciation at the large ridge between them and licked her lips, stoking the fire already blazing in his eyes.

Lightly pushing him to sit on the bed, she knelt to pull off his boots and free his legs from his jeans. He watched her every movement. Still on her knees, she came up running her hands over his thick thighs, making his muscles tense and twitch under her hands. Returning to her feet, she reached behind her back to unclasp her bra, and let it slide down her arms to the floor. Now exposed to him, he took her in, and looked up at her in awe, meeting her eyes.

"You are so beautiful," he said, his hands resting on her waist.

She smiled at him and leaned down kissing him softly but reverently. Releasing their kiss, she hooked her fingers in the sides of her underwear and slowly slid them over her hips and down her long legs, his eyes scorching a path down her body. Standing in front of him now, fully naked, her body and soul fully exposed to him, she never felt more beautiful, empowered, or desired. "Touch me," she whispered, meeting his lustful gaze. "I need your hands on me."

BEN FELT the pure need in her words, and he rose to his feet, his eyes never leaving hers. He ran his hands over her shoulders and down her bare back, her skin like silk to his touch. Swooping her into his arms, she gasped in surprise, and he smiled. Laying her out on the bed, he took a moment to take in her body with reverence. *I cannot believe she is here with me*, he thought. *Stunning.* Sliding over the length of her completely, he hovered his hot and heavy body over hers. "I want to worship you Ever."

"Please," she begged; her voice was shaky with need.

Pulling himself up to his knees straddling her body, he leaned over, capturing her lips with his in a sensual kiss, his tongue making love to her mouth. Letting his lips roam from her mouth down to her breasts peaked and ready for him, he sucked one into his mouth, making her moan out her approval. Running her hands through his hair, tugging and pulling, he devoured her breasts with fervent attention. Continuing his exploration south, he kissed down her stomach, making her pant, her body begging for more. Reaching the apex of her thighs, he caught her hungry gaze as he climbed off the bed and dropped to his knees. Pulling her to the edge, she let her knees fall open for him and he admired her, glistening, wet and rosy.

"I want to taste you, sweetheart," he confessed, lowering his head between her thighs, and sliding his tongue through her soft folds.

"Ben," Ever whimpered, lifting her hips off the bed.

Pulling her closer to him, he continued to lick, suck, and lap up every drop of her arousal till she was writhing under his ministrations. Sliding a finger into the molten heat of her body, he felt her muscles clench around it as he pumped in and out of her, his tongue lavishing attention on the bundle of nerves making her cry out in release. Trembling with pleasure, the aftershocks of her release rippling through her, she reached for him. Covering her body with his, he took in her flushed, hazy with lust face and smiled. "That was beautiful, Ever."

* * *

STILL SHAKING FROM HER ORGASM, heady desire flooding her senses, she brought him in for a searing kiss, tasting her desire on his lips. It was hopelessly sexy, and she wanted more of him. All of him.

Flipping him onto his back, she climbed onto him, straddling his legs. Running her fingers over his chest and stomach, making his muscles twitch with her touch, she ran her fingers past the waistband of his briefs, teasing him.

"Take them off." He ordered with a growl, urgency in his tone as he lifted his hips to help her.

Obeying his command, she climbed off him and slowly eased his briefs down over his hips and thighs, then off, tossing them aside. Unrestrained, her eyes widened at the sight of him. He was as large and beautiful as the rest of him. Solid as steel and powerful looking. She bit her bottom lip, giving him a look of lusty appreciation.

"You are wicked," he commented, a deep growl escaping his throat.

Darting her tongue out to wet her lips, she huskily confessed. "I want to make you feel good."

Raising up on his elbows, he watched as she ran her tongue up the length of him, circling the head with her tongue, capturing the beginnings of his arousal dripping down the underside. Her hand running up and down his length, she took him in her warm mouth, sucking him deep into her throat. He growled almost feral as she circled the head with her tongue, teasing him. He tasted musky, manly, and delicious. The sounds she elicited from him fuelling her own desire. It was heady and so hot she felt herself get wetter with each guttural sound.

"I want to be inside you, sweetheart," he growled.

She released him, still teasing him with long strokes.

"Protection?" she asked, her voice coming out breathless.

"My pocket," he rasped out huskily.

She climbed off him, finding his jeans on the floor, dug into his pocket, and pulled out the foil packet. Climbing back on top of him, she opened the packet, sliding the condom on his length, making him twitch in anticipation.

Straddling him again, she leaned down kissing him passionately while she ground her wetness over his erection.

"I want you now," he pleaded, his eyes dark and wanton.

Lifting her hips up, she positioned him at her entrance, then sank down slowly onto his solid steel. A gasp followed by a throaty moan escaped her. The size of him stretched her in painful pleasure as he filled her inch by glorious inch, making her feel impossibly full, yet somehow, as she adjusted to him, a perfect fit. She met his eyes and noticed a look of worry on his face. "You feel perfect, Bear. I promise."

His eyes softened, and he smiled as she rocked on top of him. The friction, exquisite.

* * *

BEN COULD NOT TAKE his eyes off the beautiful woman moving on top of him. Fully sheathed in the heat of her body, she felt so gloriously tight around him. She ground onto him with steady, deliberate strokes. Matching her movement, he thrust up into her, causing her to cry out in pleasure.

Riding him harder, he reached up to cup her gorgeous breasts as she chased her release. Knowing he was close, and she was with him, he flipped her over, changing positions keeping their bodies connected. Spreading her legs wider to accommodate his large body, she lifted her legs high and curled them around him giving him a deeper angle. Driving hard into her he could feel her start to crest as she cried out his name. "Just like that. Oh, Bear!"

Her pleasure fueling him, he drove faster, taking her as deep as he could, sweat beading on his skin. She convulsed and let out a husky gasp as she tumbled into ecstasy, her orgasm ripping through her body. With one more stroke, he joined her, chanting out her name. "Ever."

Stars clouded his vision as hot pleasure consumed him, making him quake with his release. The ripples of her orgasm drawing out his pleasure. Collapsing on top of her he could feel her shudder underneath him, the sweat of their skin making them both shiver. Not wanting to crush her, he rolled to his side, his breath heavy from their passionate lovemaking.

"Are you okay?" he asked, turning to Ever, her chest still heaving.

She flashed him a satisfied smile. "Yes." she whispered in a soft, raspy tone as she tried to catch her breath. "Oh, so good."

Giving her a gratified smile, he leaned over to give her a chaste kiss and rolled off the bed to dispose of the condom. Rejoining her on the bed, he wrapped his arms around her and pulled the quilt over them cocooning them in warmth. Melting into him, he marveled at how their bodies fit together so seamlessly. They lay there a few moments, just breathing together in the dark.

"What are you thinking?" he whispered in her ear, his beard tickling the side of her face as he nuzzled her neck.

"You don't want to know." she laughed, his hand cupping one breast and teasing at her nipple.

"Tell me," he urged, kneading her soft flesh with his large palm.

"I was just wondering, when can we do it again?" she confessed.

He growled in her ear and flipped the covers over their heads, making her giggle and squirm with delight.

CHAPTER 7

*E*ver's eyes opened slowly to bands of sunlight coming through her curtains, illuminating the room. Squinting at her alarm clock, it read 10:43 a.m. she smiled at the memories of the night before vividly playing back in her mind. She was sore everywhere and the thought of all they did last night suddenly made her ache for him again, both in mind and body. She had never felt so completely coveted before, and it was incredible. Feeling the wall of warmth beside her she turned herself to face him. Ben was still asleep, his lashes fanned out on his cheeks, his hair sexily disheveled. He looked peaceful and impossibly handsome. Reaching out to him, she softly brushed his hair from his eyes, running her fingers over the strong lines and ridges of his face. Gently tracing his eyebrows, she caressed down the side of his beard, running her fingers through the coarse yet soft hair.

Ben's sleepy blue eyes opened half-mast, and he smiled sleepily, his eyes crinkling in the corners as they always did.

She smiled and ran her fingertips over the creases. "I love it when you smile."

Ben grinned, eyes shining. "Good morning, sweetheart," he replied, his voice deep and raspy from sleep. "Did you sleep well?" he asked, pulling her naked body flush with his so she could rest her head on his chest.

"I did," she replied. "It's so late, Bear. We need to get up and go do the chores."

Ben smiled and squeezed her in reassurance. "I took care of it, sweetheart."

"Oh?" she asked, propping her head up to look into his eyes.

"I asked Hayden to come by and take care of it," he continued. "It's Sunday, so the Hardware Store is closed. I just heard his truck leave."

"So, you planned for him to come?" she questioned, giving him a coy smile. "That's presumptuous, Mr. Hastings. Did you know you were going to get lucky?"

"Hoped." he replied, flashing her a sexy smile.

She laughed, buried her head in his chest and curled her leg around his large body. She languidly ran her fingertips over his chest, tracing the curls of hair there and over the ridges of his stomach, reveling in the feel of his hard tight skin under her touch. *Damn, he is sexy,* she thought as she felt her body pulse with need for him. "Since we are playing hooky, what shall we do today?" she asked, pulling back the covers to reveal the rest of him.

"I can think of a few things," he offered, running his hand down her back, cupping her behind, giving it a firm squeeze.

Swinging her leg over him to straddle his hips. She

could feel him harden as she rubbed herself over the length of him. "I have a few ideas, too." She added, giving him a sexy grin, leaning over to tease his lips with her tongue.

His lips curled into a lustful smile as a husky growl rumbled from his throat.

"Am I driving you crazy, Bear?" she questioned as she deepened their kiss into a passionate embrace.

"So, fucking crazy," he replied, releasing her lips with a groan as his hands gripped her hips possessively. "I can't stop touching you."

"I don't want you to stop." She admitted as his hands ran down her back and over her backside, kneading the soft flesh feverishly.

She lifted herself to position him at her entrance and sliding down, fully sheathed him inside her.

"You feel so fucking good," he groaned as she rode his hard length in slow deliberate gyrations drawing out their pleasure. She milked him with each swivel of her hips, and she could feel him grow and thicken within her.

"I am so close, Bear." she moaned out, her eyes clouding with desire as she rode him with abandon.

He caressed her breasts, meeting her with deep thrusts, making her gasp with each one as she finally cried out his name.

"Bear! Oh God!

Ben's hands dug into her hips as he thrust deep, feeling her muscles tighten around him as her orgasm claimed her, the exquisite feel of her triggering his own release. They came together, their bodies shaking from their climaxes.

Still connected, Ever collapsed on him, breathless and satiated. She met his gratified eyes, foreheads touching, as they breathed together in unison. Ben brushed her waves of soft hair away from her face and kissed her gently.

"You are so incredibly beautiful, Ever." The tenderness in his voice was almost too much for Ever to bear. Feeling tears prick at her eyes, she took a deep breath to control her emotions as they threatened to overflow. "Are you okay?" he asked, searching her eyes in concern.

"Just never had anyone look at me the way you do," she confessed.

He smiled and caressed her cheek softly as he drew her in for another soul-searching kiss. Wrapping her in his arms, she felt his heartbeat strong and steady, and she felt truly safe and content for the first time in her life.

HUNGER DEMANDING, they rolled out of bed, Ben slipping on his boxers and Ever, slipping into his dress shirt. Smiling in approval, he wrapped his powerful arms around her.

"You look so sexy wearing my shirt," he growled, nipping her ear with his teeth.

"Stop!" she chided with a giggle, wriggling from his arms, and gesturing for him to come with her. "Let's get something to eat."

Descending the stairs, they made their way into the kitchen. Looking through the fridge, Ever retrieved a pint of strawberries and looked up at him. What would you like?"

"I want to cook for you," he insisted, taking out a long griddle and firing up the burners on the gas stove.

With approval, she handed him the berries and took a seat on the kitchen table, feet dangling off the edge.

Retrieving pancake mix from the cupboard, a mixing bowl, whisk and milk from the fridge, he quickly whipped up the batter. Pouring big ladles onto the hot griddle. Finding a colander, he washed the strawberries and put them in a bowl for Ever.

Happily, she took one and put it to her lips, taking a big bite of the juicy fruit. A moan escaped her throat, making Ben turn to her with a sexy grin. He shook his head, bringing his attention back to their breakfast.

"So, did you notice we didn't use protection this morning?" she asked, taking another bite of her berry as she watched for his reaction.

He turned to her, spatula in hand, his eyes wide.

"I didn't," he confessed with a look of concern on his face. "We got a little carried away."

She smiled at him playfully, nodding in agreement.

"It's okay, Bear, I am on birth control. I'm okay going without if you are?"

Ben strode over to her, nestling himself between her legs and running his hands over her thighs. "Are you sure, sweetheart?" he asked, searching her eyes.

"I trust you."

Ben's eyes softened, and he brushed his lips over hers. He tasted the sweetness of the berries as she sucked in his bottom lip and let it go with a pop. "You are going to make me want to take you right here on this table." He growled out.

"What's stopping you?" she teased, putting another berry to her lips, mischief dancing in her eyes.

He flashed her a sexy grin, growled and grabbed the rest of the berry from her hand with his teeth, making her giggle with delight.

"Your pancakes are burning," she observed, looking past his shoulder to the smoking griddle behind him.

Quickly turning to see his first batch of pancakes ruined, he laughed. "You are too distracting!"

She gave him a wink as she watched him start another batch, spatula in hand, watching this batch, careful not to burn them. Sliding off the table, she set down the strawberries and went about the task of making a pot of coffee. Before long, they were sitting together at the table enjoying a delicious stack of warm pancakes smothered in butter and syrup. After a few delicious bites, she looked up at Ben with mischief in her eyes.

"So, besides being a sex god, you can cook too?" she asked, her eyebrow raised in question.

Ben nearly spit out his coffee and started to laugh. "I'm glad you are happy with…" he trailed off. "The sex? The food?"

"Both." she replied playfully, reaching out and wiping a little dab of butter off his beard, then licking it off her finger.

Ben took her hand and kissed her palm affectionately. "I am happy with you."

EVER SETTLED in next to Ben on the worn leather living room couch, a thin blanket covering their bare legs. With a hand on his chest, she met his lazy gaze and stretched to kiss his soft lips sweetly. Happy and contented, she sighed as he pulled her into him, his arms enrobing her with warmth.

Glancing behind him to the easel and canvas by the window, he asked curiously. "Have you found your inspiration yet?"

Shaking her head, she followed his gaze and exhaled with resolve. "Not yet. I'm not sure what is wrong with me."

Meeting her gaze with empathy in his eyes, he kissed her on the head to reassure her. "You will find your inspiration, sweetheart. I am sure it's there. You just need to find it again."

She nodded and nestled back into him, quiet falling on them as they held each other. Breaking their revery Ben spoke, "I would love to see the paintings you have done. Do you have pictures?" he asked with genuine interest.

Ever's head popped up, and she brightened. Excitedly, she slid off the couch and padded into the front entrance retrieving her purse still on the floor. Pulling out her phone, she returned to the couch. Sitting up fully, Ben pulled her onto his lap as she curled up and opened her phone to find her photo gallery. Scrolling down, she stopped and handed her phone to Ben, gesturing for him to swipe left. With interest, he slowly scrolled through her photos and met her anxious gaze.

"Wow, Ever! These are beautiful! You are incredibly talented!" he beamed with adoration.

"Thank you. I am proud of my work."

Continuing to scroll, Ben stopped on a picture and furrowed his brow. Peeking over the phone, Ever brightened to see which of her paintings caught his attention. "That is one of my favorites! It's the first painting I ever sold."

The picture was a serene scene in a park, with a white bench and beautiful purple flowers in the background. The painting looked like it was in soft focus, giving it an ethereal, dreamlike quality.

"I've seen this painting before." he confessed, meeting her gaze.

"Oh?" she inquired in surprise.

"Did your dad ever see your paintings?" he asked, his eyes boring into hers.

"Sadly no, I don't think so," she replied, regret etched on her face. "I did a few pieces in high school, but I did not start painting seriously until I was accepted into Art School. By the time I left for Toronto, my dad and I were not talking."

"Follow me," he said, lifting Ever off his lap and setting her down on her feet. Her phone still in his hand, he rose from the couch and took her hand leading her to the sliding door of her father's office. "Do you mind?" he asked, gesturing to the sliding door.

"No, go ahead. I haven't been able to go in there yet," she confessed.

Sliding the door open, Ben looked around eagerly, zoning in on his target. Facing her father's desk on the wall near the corner above his favorite recliner was her painting.

Ever cupped her mouth with a gasp. "It's my painting." She murmured in disbelief.

Coming up behind her, Ben wrapped his supportive arms around her waist, holding her close to him as they stared at the painting. "I asked him once about it and he said it reminded him of his late wife, your mom. He never told me you painted it, though."

"He bought my first painting." She whispered, her voice breaking as tears filled her eyes and spill down her cheeks.

Turning her to face him, she sank her face into his chest. He wiped the tears from her face tenderly as he held her close to him. His warmth comforted her as she cried. Her heart was broken for the years she lost with her father.

CHAPTER 8

It was mid-afternoon and the soft light from the picture window cast shadows on the wall. Ben held her wrapped in a blanket, his arms around her protectively. Her tears had subsided, and they lay together in silent contemplation. It broke Ben's heart to see her cry, feeling his chest tighten as she let out all the pain and hurt she was carrying. Despite the ache in his heart, he held her and consoled her, knowing she needed his strength right now. Having lost his own parents, he could relate in many ways, but he could not understand the distance that had existed between Ever and her father. Would she ever get answers? He didn't know. But one thing he did know was that he could be here for her and help her navigate through this. He kissed away the remaining tears that lingered on her cheeks, and she smiled at him appreciatively. She kissed him softly, her embrace so grateful and tender his heart swelled.

"Did you want to go for a walk or perhaps take a drive

with me? I can show you where I live," he suggested, knowing she would probably appreciate a distraction.

"Do I have to get dressed?" she asked, lifting the blanket to expose her bare legs and body still covered in his oversized shirt.

He laughed with a mischievous twinkle in his eye. "As much as I love to see you in my shirt and would love to keep you naked all day, yes, I think clothes may be a good idea."

Ever nodded, a grin on her face. She slid off his lap, stood and stretched. Turning to take his hand, she tried to pull him up, laughing, realizing there was no way she was going to make him budge. He smiled as she crashed back into him, and they laughed together. Conceding, he swooped her up in his arms, planted a chaste kiss on her lips and carried her up the stairs, her giggle echoing through the house.

Quickly they dressed. Ben slipping on his clothes from the night before, and Ever pulling on a short jean skirt, white Bon Jovi concert t-shirt, jean jacket and red Chucks. She pulled her hair up into a messy ponytail and he admired her in the full-length mirror. "Damn, you look cute!" he complimented as he spun her around and kissed her passionately. Releasing her, she giggled and wrapped her arms around him in a hug. "Pizza and a movie at my place?"

* * *

SEEING the Primrose town sign come into view, Ever smiled. She had been back in Primrose for a few weeks now and she had not realized how much she missed it. No matter where she landed in life, Primrose always felt like home and that realization made her happy. Happier than she had been a long time, if she was being honest with herself. Glancing at Ben, she knew he was the reason why. Ben felt like home.

Ben pulled his truck into the parking lot of the Eazy Café and Gas Bar and they both got out of the cab, meeting at the front of the truck. Stopping her, he flashed her a smile and intertwined his hand with hers.

"You realize when we go in there, everyone is going to start talking, right?" she informed him.

"Let them talk." he shrugged without worry. "I can handle the talk. If anyone asks, I will say we are seeing each other."

"So, like your girlfriend?" she asked in clarification.

"Do you want to be?" he asked, volleying back to her.

Ever stopped and put her crooked finger to her chin, tapping it in thought, and glanced at him playfully. "I guess it's better than calling me your LOVER." she enunciated the word, drawing it out.

Ben laughed and pulled her into him to tickle her sides. She giggled and squirmed. "Yes, I will be your girl-friend, Bear."

Ben leaned down to kiss her softly and took her hand again as they made their way inside the Eazy together. They made their way to the back of the store to the video rental section, browsing the rows for some-thing that looked interesting. Whispers around them made them chuckle as they agreed on a romantic comedy.

"I'm going to go get our pizza. Pepperoni fine?" he asked.

She nodded in agreement as she continued to peruse the back of one of the movie cases.

Suddenly, fingers poked her sides, startling her. She turned around to see Bea, clad in her work scrubs, hip cocked to the side and a look of "Where the hell have you been?" on her face. Amused, Ever smiled at her friend and shrugged with a laugh. Bea was so dramatic.

"I have been worried sick about you, young lady!" Bea scolded with a twinkle in her eye. "What have you been up to? Or should I ask, who have you been "UP" with?" she air quoted.

Ever glanced over to the pizza counter where Ben stood looking devilishly handsome as he waited for their pizza. He looked up, noticing Bea was with Ever and gave them one of his dashing smiles with a two-finger wave.

Bea looked from Ben to Ever, and back to Ben again. "No fucking way." she whispered, pulling Ever into a corner. "So, you have bedded the big boy?" she asked, thrilled with this new tidbit of knowledge.

Ever laughed at her friend's reference and nodded, knowing it was futile to keep secrets from her best friend. Bea squealed loudly with delight and then covered her mouth, knowing she was drawing attention to them. Ever laughed and flashed her a "be quiet" look.

"Details." Bea urged, keeping her voice down. "I need details."

"What are you two taking about?" Ben interrupted, holding a large pizza box.

Both girls giggled like teenagers and Bea looked up at

Ben deadpan. "Just talking about your HUGE...." Bea started before Ever gave her a punch in the arm and her cheeks reddened in embarrassment. "Heart." Bea finished, flashing them both a playful smile. "What did you think I was going to say?"

Ben let out a deep, hearty laugh and shook his head. Classic Bea. "Are you coming from work or headed to work?" he asked, pointing to her scrubs, and referring to her job as an Emergency Department Nurse at St. Augustine Regional Hospital.

"Headed to work. Was just filling up my car when I spotted you two. So, this is a thing now?" she asked, pointing to the two of them.

"It is." Ben replied, slipping his arms around Ever from behind and kissing her cheek.

Bea smiled approvingly and laughed, "It's about damn time!"

* * *

BEN PULLED up to a 1970s build bungalow with a red and brown brick façade and double wide garage. Window boxes planted with colorful wave petunias gave the otherwise plain exterior a nice welcoming touch. The yard was nicely groomed and the flower beds were clean and neat.

"Wow, so this is your place. It's nice!" she brightened in surprise. "I was expecting a total bachelor pad!"

Ben laughed, looking around. "We try to keep it nice. My mom took a lot of pride in her gardening. So, we try for her."

"I know you said your parents had passed. How long ago?" she asked, sympathy in her eyes.

"It was three years in January. They died in a car accident. Uncontrolled intersection," he reflected with sadness. "I am grateful each day they did not suffer, and that they went together. They were each other's worlds, best friends. Not sure one could have survived without the other."

"How long were they married?"

"33 years."

Ever gave Ben a smile of appreciation and he nodded in agreement.

"How old were you when your mom passed away?" he asked.

"About two years old, I think. My dad raised me alone. I don't know much about her, to be honest. Dad was not forthcoming and when I would ask about her, as a child, he would either change the subject or just say she was his everything." She shared. "By the time I was a teenager, I stopped asking. Not having grandparents still alive that I could remember or any aunts or uncles, I did not have anyone to ask either. It's sort of a mystery to me."

"So, you never saw pictures of her?" Ben asked, his eyebrows furrowed.

"Just the one on the mantel at the Farmhouse. She is sitting on the front steps of the porch, a large bright smile, hair the same color as mine. We look very much alike from what I can tell. I would sometimes catch my dad holding the picture to his chest, but he would never say anything about her. One thing I do know is he loved her very much." she said with a smile. "I have this hope that going through the house will provide me with answers. But I still have not gone through his room or the office."

"Why do you think that is?" Ben asked.

"Not sure exactly." She shrugged. "Perhaps I fear what I might find. I don't know."

"Do you want me to help you?" he offered, unbuckling his seat belt.

"Would you? It is so much to go through! I kind of don't know where to begin." she cringed with a frown.

Taking Ever's hand, he squeezed it. "Anything you need. Just ask, okay?"

Ever leaned over and gave him a grateful kiss. "Thank you."

Exiting the truck, Ever took the pizza box from Ben so he could unlock the door.

"After you." He gestured, placing his hand on the small of her back as she stepped inside his home.

The front entrance was small, with hooks for jackets and a wooden bench with space underneath for shoes and boots. Immediately to the right was a large casual living room with a huge sectional, 50-inch television mounted on the wall across from it and a large coffee table holding remotes, magazines, and a few books. To the left was a hallway that Ben explained led to the bedrooms and bathroom. Ben explained that Hayden had his own space in the fully finished basement. Guiding her to the kitchen, she took in the light wood cabinets, white quartz countertops, stainless steel appliances and island / breakfast bar with seating for four. The eat in kitchen looked modern and inviting, obviously having been renovated from the original.

Grabbing two plates from the cupboard, Ben reached into the fridge and grabbed two sodas, offering one to Ever. She took it and followed him into the living room with the pizza box. Ever settled into the couch and Ben offered her a plate with a few slices of pizza. Joining her on the couch, plate in hand he cued up the movie they rented with the remote.

"Jerry Maguire?" he questioned, one eyebrow raised.

She laughed, knowing this was probably not his first choice.

"I have never seen it," he confessed.

"What?" she squawked back at him in disbelief. "It's a classic! And it has the best movie line ever!"

"We'll see," he said playfully, putting his arm around her and giving her a wink as he took a bite of his pizza.

Giving him a pat on the stomach, she laughed. "I promise you will like it, Bear."

Two hours later, Ben sat quietly on the couch, Ever's sleeping head lay softly in his lap. She had missed the last half hour of the movie, and he did not have the heart to wake her. She breathed deeply as she slept. Running his fingers over the escaping tendrils of her ponytail, he stroked her hair tenderly as his mind wandered off to their earlier conversation about her father and mother. *I hope Ever finds answers.*

A flashback of a conversation he had shared with Hardin a few years ago suddenly came to mind. He had finished a day's work and peeked into the barn office to find Hardin sitting in his office chair. He held a small wallet size picture in his hand. Noticing Ben, he smiled and gestured for him to come into the office and take a seat. Ben sat across from him and he handed him the picture he was holding. The picture was of a woman in her early 30s, pale skin, head covered by a colorful scarf. She looked frail but had kind, smiling eyes. Next to her was a pretty little girl in a pink sundress, wispy reddish-brown hair, rosy cheeks, and a shy smile. He looked to Hardin, raising his eyebrows in question.

"That was the last day I had with her." Hardin shared.

Ben flipped over the picture and written on the back were the names Violet and Daisy.

Ben handed it back to Hardin, and his mouth went into a grim line.

"She had cancer."

Not wanting to say more, Hardin cleared his throat, got up from his seat and tucked the picture into his wallet.

The sound of the key in the front door broke him out of his memory. Glancing behind him, he saw Hayden slipping inside.

"Hey there Ben!" he exclaimed then quickly quieted, noticing Ever asleep on Ben's lap. He gave Ben a mischievous grin and asked. "Did you tire her out?"

Scowling at Hayden, he growled under his breath at his brother's inference. Hayden laughed quietly, rolling his eyes and put his hand on his brother's shoulder.

"Seriously though, bro, I am happy for you."

Ben smiled, then looked down at the beautiful woman he knew he was falling for.

* * *

EVER STIRRED and opened her eyes. Disoriented, she looked around realizing she had fallen asleep. Ben's large hand was on her shoulder and her head was buried in his lap, a soft blanket over her legs. She felt warm and safe.

"Hey." a deep voice whispered.

Looking up, she met Ben's tender gaze and gave him a sleepy smile. "Did I fall asleep?" she asked, sitting up, yawning, and bowing her back in a stretch.

He nodded his answer as he reached over to massage her shoulders, eliciting a sigh of pleasure.

"Did I miss the end of the movie?" she asked, turning to him with a pouty frown.

"You did, but I saw the end."

"Did you like it?" her lips curved into a smile. "Wasn't that the best line ever?"

"You had me at hello? Yeah, it was pretty good!" he admitted, feigning indifference.

She smiled and climbed onto his lap, straddling him and bringing her arms around his neck. He smoothed the stray hairs escaping from her ponytail and looked deep into her eyes. Leaning down she kissed him softly at first, then deepened their kiss, their tongues tangling sensually. As their kiss became heated, his hands roamed over her bare legs and under her jean skirt to cup her behind. Expertly, he rose from the couch, lifting her with him. Her legs still wrapped around his body; he carried her down the dark hallway to his bedroom. Tossing her down on the bed, she giggled as he came over her possessively caging her in. The all-consuming heat of his body melting her into the mattress. Holding himself over her, he kissed her long and deep, making her body crave his touch. Releasing their passionate embrace, he trailed kisses down her neck, the friction of his beard making her writhe underneath him.

"Did you want to spend the night?" he asked, meeting her hooded gaze.

She nodded, crashing her lips to his again in a hungry kiss. Breathlessly releasing him, she continued, "But I could use a shower."

"So could I." Ben smiled wickedly as he stood up and unbuttoned his shirt, removing it and throwing it into a hamper in the corner. "Mind if I join you?" he asked, gesturing to the open door of the ensuite bathroom.

Ever smiled, running her hands over his hard chest and down his swoon worthy abs in appreciation. Looking up at him through her lashes, giving him a flirtatious grin, she asked, "You wash my back and I wash yours?"

"Something like that," he responded, matching her flirtation as he lifted her shirt over her head.

"Perfect." she replied, unbuttoning her skirt slowly and sliding it down over her curves. Ben growled and quickly shed his jeans. Seductively meeting his gaze, she reached behind her back, unclasping her bra, then slowly slid her panties down her legs, leaving her fully exposed to him. He licked his lips and quickly removed his underwear, almost tripping as he tried to get out of them. Ever giggled at his struggle and Ben, now naked, stalked over to her, swooping her into his arms and carrying her into the bathroom.

Setting her down in his large standing shower, he

started the water, taking care to turn the spray away from her while it warmed. Stepping in with his hand on her waist to steady them, he reached for the body wash and squirted some in his hands bringing them together creating suds. He smoothed his hands over her shoulders, massaging as he went, then down her back, eliciting a deep moan from her throat.

"That feels amazing," She cooed as his hands roamed over to her breasts, stopping to gently caress them, giving attention to their pebbled peaks. He slid his large hands lower over her ribs, down the skin of her supple belly, and between her legs.

"Ben." she whispered out huskily as he caressed languidly between her folds. Closing her eyes, she could feel her desire pool with each delicious stroke of his fingers.

Shivering, he positioned her under the warm spray, washing away the soap as he kissed her passionately, his tongue darting to meet hers. Breaking their embrace, Ever took a handful of soap and started washing his body.

"Your turn," she offered as she ran her hands over his sinewy shoulders and back and over his magnificent backside, giving it a squeeze. He growled in approval as she slid her hands down his washboard abs and over the solid steel length of him. Running her hands up and down over his shaft, making him groan in pleasure. Surprising her, he stopped her hand and lifted both her arms above her head, pinning her to the wall of the shower with his hard, heavy body, his eyes dark and intense with lust. She gasped and moaned as he possessively held her there and took one of her breasts in his mouth, ravaging them in turn then tugging at the nipple gently with his teeth. She was lost, primal moans escaping involuntarily. Releasing her hands, he flipped her around, his front to her back and ground into her body as he cupped and teased her breasts. She felt like lava under his touch. Melting into the sensations he was eliciting. Sliding his hand down her back, he slid his hands over her behind, kneading her round globes.

"Hands on the wall and lean forward," he ordered.

Hungry with lust, she obeyed, enjoying this alpha side of him she had not fully seen yet. She bent forward, and he smoothed his hands over her back, then gripping her hips, he plunged into her depths in one swift move. She cried out in pleasure, bracing herself on the wall as he drove into her with long deep strokes, making her entire body shudder with desire.

"Does that feel good, sweetheart?" he asked between demanding thrusts.

"Yes!" she cried out. "So good!"

Feeling her orgasm building, she urged him by pushing back. "Bear please." She begged. "Faster, harder, please."

Digging his fingers into the sides of her hips, he thrusted punishingly into her, the sound of their wet skin slapping and deep feral moans echoing from them both. Feeling her orgasm peak, she screamed out in pleasure in a long-drawn-out cry.

"Oh Fuck!" Ben growled as the spasms of her muscles milked every ounce of pleasure from him, making him lose sense of time a place for a moment as his movements slowed and his own release ripped through him. Coming down and still connected, he wrapped his arms around Ever's waist, bringing her back to his chest and kissed her neck as they caught their breaths under the shower spray. "Are you okay?" he whispered hoarsely, knowing how hard he had just taken her body.

"How can it always be so good?" she asked with a nod, trembling under his touch.

His lips brushed her ear. "I have never had it so good," he confessed, engulfing her in his arms.

Ever turned her body to face him and shivered, noticing the water was running cold.

"Let's get you out of here," he offered as they did another quick rinse off and climbed out of the shower.

Ben wrapped her in a fluffy towel and rubbed her shoulders to warm her, giving her an affectionate kiss on the forehead. Grabbing a towel for himself and wrapping it around his hips, they re-entered his bedroom.

Stealing a moment to fully take in his bedroom, Ever let out a little laugh seeing his huge king size bed with a beautiful carved headboard. "A big bed for a big man!" she teased, wiggling her eyebrows.

Whipping off his towel, he wound it up to swat her. It cracked against her thigh, and she giggled, jumping onto the bed. He tackled her playfully pinning her to the mattress with his strong naked body hovering over hers. Wiping the wet hair from her face, he reached down to unwrap her towel and kissed her so tenderly she felt her heart flutter wildly. Feeling him harden between them, she looked at him with wide eyes. "Ready again so soon, Mr. Hastings?"

He grinned back at her mischievously and shrugged deadpan. "Sex god, you know."

She smiled as her knees fell to the side, letting him sink into her once more. As he made love to her, this time slowly and tenderly, she knew then and there that he had made his way into her heart, and she was starting to fall.

CHAPTER 9

As May rolled into June, the days grew hotter, and so did their relationship. Spending their days hard at work on the farm, drinking Sun Tea on the porch and making love every night. They explored each other's bodies with abandon, discovering all the ways they could wring pleasure from each other. They settled into a blissful existence together, both never having been so contented and happy.

Despite Ever's euphoric state, the decision on the future of the farm loomed over her. Still unsure of the right course to take, she decided it was finally time to go through her father's belongings. Entering his bedroom, it felt strange to be around his things. Being a private man, her father's bedroom was his sanctuary. Even as a child, Ever seldom was in his space.

Looking around, she took in the large room with its simple oak bed and dresser. Her father liked simple things and never felt the need for fancy furnishings.

She put two boxes down on the bed and walked over

to the dresser, running her hands over its smooth top. A small glass bowl held his watch, a silver dollar, and his Swiss Army knife. Turning to the bed again, she noticed one of his plaid work shirts hanging over the footboard. Picking it up, she held it to her nose. The sweet smell of Old Spice cologne enveloped her senses. She smiled, remembering how he would ask for a bottle every Christmas. A man of simple pleasures. Folding the shirt, she set it in a box marked "KEEP". Glancing over to the bedside table she noticed her father's wallet. She sat down on the bed and held it in her hands. The soft, worn leather had seen better days. She opened it, seeing the usual receipts, two twenty-dollar bills, a debit card for the local Credit Union, and a few pictures. Pulling out the pictures, she sifted through them, smiling as she took in each one. Several of her grade school photos, her graduation photo and an old black & white photo of her late grandparents were there. Continuing to sift through them, she stopped and squinted at the photo in her hands. The picture was of a woman around her age smiling at the camera. She looked pale, very frail with dark circles under her eyes, her cheeks slightly concave, making her dark eyes stand out. Her head was wrapped in a colorful scarf and, despite her obviously ill appearance, her smile matched its cheerfulness. A little rosy-cheeked girl sat beside her looking shyly at the camera. She held it up to the light coming through the window, trying to place the pair in the picture. As she was doing this, she heard Ben's heavy footsteps on the stairs.

"Ever!" he called.

"In my dad's room!"

Coming around the corner, Ben leaned on the door frame, watching her. "What are you doing?" he asked, entering the room, and taking a seat next to her on the bed.

"Going through my dad's things." She replied, eyes still transfixed on the photo. "I found this strange picture in his wallet."

Handing the photo to him, he nodded knowingly. "It's your mom."

"How do you know?" she inquired; brows furrowed.

"A few years ago, your dad showed it to me. I was surprised when he did because, as you know, he was not the most forthcoming man. He told me it was taken just before she passed." he offered, giving the picture back to her. "He said she had cancer."

Ever's eyes widened, taking in the picture again and turning it over reading, *Violet and Daisy*. "Daisy?" Ever questioned. "Who's Daisy?"

"I assumed it was you in the picture. Did he ever call you that? Perhaps it was a nickname or a name your mom liked to call you?"

Ever shrugged, shaking her head. "No, never."

"Hardin seemed to have had a lot of things he kept to himself." Ben resolved. "Perhaps we should tackle his office this weekend. Maybe we will find some answers in there."

Ever nodded and held the picture to her chest. Putting his arm around her, Ben pulled her in for a hug and kissed her head. "We will figure everything out, I promise you."

* * *

WITH HER FAMILY mysteries still unfolding, Ever decided she needed to investigate further. Pulling up to the library in Primrose, she entered the building and was immediately greeted by the town librarian, Ms. Lynette.

"Ever darlin', where have you been?" she greeted, opening her arms and inviting Ever in for a big hug. Ms. Lynette was a short stout woman in her mid 60s. Her silver hair perfectly coiffed in a bouncy bob and her signature cat's eyeglasses framing her bright blue eyes, she wore a light blue polka dot dress with white sneakers. Not the stereotypical librarian garb, but quintessentially Ms. Lynette.

Ever loved coming to the library when she lived in Primrose. Ms. Lynette always greeted her with hugs and a million questions, wanting to know everything going on with her. In some ways, Ms. Lynette took on a motherly role for her and she appreciated her genuine interest in her life.

"I hear you and that sweet Ben Hastings are an item." she winked playfully, giving her a nudge.

On top of being the town librarian, Ms. Lynette was the self-proclaimed town busybody. Nary a tidbit of gossip missed her ears and if you wanted to know the scoop, or who was up to what, she was the one to go to.

"Yes, Ben and I have been seeing each other." she laughed, knowing there was no way to deny it.

"Oh, thank heavens!" she exclaimed. "A handsome strapping man like that, so smart and hardworking. Such a great catch! Goodness, I was getting worried about him!"

"I will let him know about your concern for him." Ever

replied with a hearty laugh. Looking around, Ever asked. "Do you have any old newspapers here? I am looking for something specific."

"Sure! Everything is online." Ms. Lynette informed taking her to a computer. "What years are you looking for?"

"1979 and 1993 to 1994."

Showing Ever where to find the newspaper records, she left her alone to search. Searching 1979 first, she quickly found an engagement announcement.

WOLTON – SCHARPENSKI

Clarence and Vivian Scharpenski announce the engagement of their daughter, Violet Scharpenski to Hardin Wolton, son of Everett and Beth Wolton, both of Primrose. The couple are planning a summer wedding, with the ceremony to be held at Primrose United Church and a reception at the Wolton family farm, Prairie Sky Acres.

A black and white picture of her parents accompanied the announcement. The recognizable but much younger face of her father and a beautiful young woman with wavy long hair, large eyes, and a bright smile. Even with the black and white picture, she could see her resemblance to her mother.

"Ms. Lynette?"

"Yes, darlin!" she peeked from around a bookcase.

"Can I print out a few things?"

"Sure can! Just hit print and it will come up on the printer behind the desk. When you are done, let me know and I will give you your printouts."

Nodding, Ever continued her search, typing 1993 into the search engine. Combing the obituaries, she came up empty, then searched 1994. Just when she wondered if she would find what she was looking for, her mother's obituary popped up on the screen.

VIOLET WOLTON (Nee Scharpenski) April 4, 1961 - June 28, 1994

Violet Emily Wolton passed away June 28, 1994, at the age of 33 after a short battle with cancer. Violet is survived by her loving husband, Hardin Wolton, her daughter Daisy Wolton, and her parents Clarence and Vivian Scharpenski. As a devoted wife and mother, Violet loved life on the farm. She loved art and loved to draw, often being seen with her sketchbook in hand. She will be remembered for her warm and generous spirit, her smile that lit up every room, and her kindness to everyone. Everyone was family to Violet and her loss is felt by all lucky enough to know her. A Celebration of Life is to be held at Primrose United Church on July 2nd at 2 p.m., with a private burial to follow.

Ever hit print and read it over again. Her mother was an artist too. She mused at their commonalities, feeling an overwhelming sense of closeness to her late mother. Satisfied with her research, she got up from the computer and met Ms. Lynette at the front desk. "I think I am done for now."

Ms. Lynette nodded and reached down to hand her the papers she had printed. Glancing down, she noticed what Ever had printed. "Did you find everything you were looking for?" she asked, eyebrows raised in question.

"For now, yes." Ever replied with thanks as she turned to leave. Suddenly a thought struck her, so she turned back to Ms. Lynette. "You knew my dad when he was younger, right?"

"Sure did! We grew up together, went to the same schools as well." She offered.

"Did you know my mother?" Ever asked hopefully.

A look of sadness and regret covered Ms. Lynette's face. "I did," she answered simply. "Such a tragedy. She was so wonderful, and your dad loved her so much!"

"Can I ask you about her?" she inquired; eyes eager to know more. "Dad would never share anything, and honestly until recently I had no idea she died from cancer."

Smiling up at her with kind eyes, Ms. Lynette put her hand on Ever's and spoke. "I thought you would never ask. How much time do you have, Darlin'?"

* * *

RETURNING HOME after the discovery of the afternoon, papers in hand, she noticed Ben was unloading feed from the back of his truck. Seeing her walking up the path, he stopped, removed his cap, and wiped the sweat from his brow.

"Hey Sweetheart. Where have you been?" he inquired curiously.

"I made a quick trip into town to see Ms. Lynette," she responded, waving the papers in her hands.

"How is that old girl?" he laughed as he picked up

another bag of feed and heaved it onto his shoulders, carrying it into the barn.

"Worried about you, apparently!" she shouted after him. "Your love-life has been of great concern to her!"

Reappearing through the barn door, he let out a deep baritone chuckle. "Yes, she has told me that before."

"Ms. Lynette is something else!" she laughed as she shook her head.

"So, I assume you were doing some investigating if you were at the library?"

"Yes, I found some info on my parents, actually." she said, taking a seat on the tailgate.

Ben, taking out a bandana, wiped his face and took a seat beside her. "What did you find out?" he asked, taking off his work gloves and setting them down beside him.

She handed over the papers she had printed out and Ben perused them. Eyebrows raised; he handed them back to her.

"Ms. Lynette also shared a lot of info with me. She grew up with my parents and apparently, they used to double date with Ms. Lynette and her late husband Fred. As she put it, they were the best of friends."

"Wow!" Ben exclaimed. "Did you ever know this?"

"Kind of. I mean, I knew my dad and Ms. Lynette knew each other from childhood and she and her late husband would come around to visit with us from time to time. But honestly, I had no idea they were so close." she shrugged.

Nodding, Ben glanced toward her, wanting to know more.

"She told me that my parents were married very young

and were completely head over heels in love." she smiled thoughtfully. "They waited to start a family because they were so young, but a few years later, they started one. Apparently, they tried for a long time and finally after eight years, I came into the world."

"That is a long time." Ben commented.

"Yeah. Shortly after I was born, she got sick and was diagnosed with Uterine Cancer. After surgeries, they thought she was in remission until about a year later, when she got sick again. The cancer had spread to other organs and by then no treatment could be done. She passed away shortly thereafter." she shared, staring off into the distance. "I was only about 18 months old."

Glancing at her with sad eyes, Ben took her hand in his to encourage her to continue.

"Ms. Lynette said my dad was devastated and literally shut everyone out. For a year, my mother's parents, my grandparents, had to step in to take care of me, as my father could hardly take care of himself. Apparently, during this time, he almost lost the farm. Only with the kindness of neighbours was he able to keep it going."

Letting that info sink in, Ben ran his hand over his face and beard. "Depression?" he asked, giving her a concerned look.

"I don't know, exactly, but yes, it sounds like it was," she answered truthfully. "Ms Lynette said it was not until my grandparents threatened to take me home to live with them permanently that he finally stepped up again to take on his responsibilities."

Ben shook his head in disbelief. "I guess you were too young to remember any of this."

"All I ever remember was me and my dad. Two against the world, as he would say." Ever looked over at Ben, sadness in her eyes. "I found out about Daisy too.", she continued.

"Oh?" he looked up in curiosity, meeting her eyes.

"You were right. I am Daisy Wolton."

WITH PUZZLE PIECES slowly coming together, Ever was determined to find the answers she needed. There was only one place she could think of that might provide them: her father's office.

Walking into her father's office, she rounded the desk and took a seat in the office chair. She sifted through the papers on his desk. They were all invoices for farm expenses, receipts, and typical farm business paperwork with a few livestock magazines in the mix. Nothing out of the ordinary. Pulling out the desk drawers, she found nothing abnormal, basically office supplies. Zoning in on the tall metal filing cabinet in the corner, she stood up and noticed the cabinet was locked.

"Where would he keep the key?" she whispered. "His key ring, yes!"

Heading back into the front entrance and reaching into the bowl sitting on the narrow table, her father's keys were still there. Grabbing them, she made her way back into his office and fumbled through the keys until she found the one that fit the lock. The file cabinet now unlocked; she opened it slowly to see the usual hanging file system. She sifted through the files, going through each file folder, most containing tax information with receipts and invoices. One folder marked legal documents caught her attention, so she pulled it out, bringing it to the desk. Taking a seat in the leather office chair, she looked through each document. The deed for the farm, a copy of his Will, a surveyor's certificate for the property and the last document, making Ever stop, her hands trembling. A clue.

"Application for the Change of Name."

Ever skimmed the document. September 4, 1994 - Change of name from Daisy Everleigh Wolton to Ever Bethany Wolton.

Confusion washed over her face as she sat back in the chair, her head spinning with questions. *Why would my father legally change my name?* She silently asked as she read through the document again.

"Daddy, why so many secrets?" she whispered as she stood up and stared at her painting on his office wall.

Glancing down to her father's recliner in the corner, she spotted a faded leather journal on the seat. *Was that there before?* Picking it up, she unbound the leather tie that held it together and took a seat in the recliner. Closing her eyes, the scent of Old Spice and the soft material of the chair felt like a hug. A hug from her father. Returning her attention to the journal, she ran her hands over the cover, tracing the lines deep in the leather. It was old. Worn and frayed on the edges. Something her father probably treasured. Slowly she opened it to see, written on the first page, in her father's handwriting, "Journal of Hardin Wolton."

CHAPTER 10

*E*xcerpts from the Journal of Hardin Wolton:

MAY 28, 1977

I am not sure where she came from, but today, I think, I met an angel. Pulling up to Primrose Feeds this morning, I saw her. Sitting on the edge of the loading dock, bare feet dangling and a sketchbook in hand. She was so beautiful. Long wavy red brown hair and large brown eyes. The kind of eyes you could get lost in if you looked into them too long. When I got out of the truck, she looked up at me and smiled. Her smile made my heart jump. The prettiest girl I have ever seen. I asked Will, as he loaded my feed onto the truck, who she was, and he said she is the owner of the feed mill's daughter. She is 16, so one year younger than me. I will look for her at school. I need to know more about her and see her again.

. . .

MAY 30, 1977

Today I looked for her at school and it did not take long to find her in the library with her sketchbook beside her. I sat down with my copy of "Catcher in the Rye" at her table, and she looked up at me. She smiled and asked me, "Do you like J. D. Salinger?" I nodded, and she introduced herself. Her name is Violet. Such a pretty name. We talked about our favorite books, and she showed me a sketch she was working on. Then I walked her to her next class. We decided to meet in the library again tomorrow. I want to ask her out the first chance I get.

APRIL 7, 1978

All I want is to spend my days with Violet. Violet helps me with my chores so we can spend more time together going to movies in St. Augustine, reading together on the porch and taking long drives in the country. We park at the dead end near the diversion and kiss. Her lips are so soft, and I cannot get enough of her. I want more with her, but I am a gentleman. Violet wants to wait till marriage, and I know and respect it. I love her very much. She consumes my every thought and I want to be the man to marry her. When I graduate in June and am going to ask her father's blessing to ask her to marry me. I hope he says yes.

AUGUST 2, 1978

She said yes! I asked her during the Pioneer Days fireworks. Our parents were there, as well as Fred & Lynette. Her father gave me his blessing but asked that we wait until Violet graduates to get married. We have one year to wait and make plans for our future. Violet wants to move to the farm after we are married, so she can stay close to her family in Primrose. I want her here with me, too. Mom and Dad are talking about retiring next spring and want to pass the farm on to me. It's a lot of work, but I know I can handle it. My whole life has been the farm until Violet came along. I will do my parents proud and be the best husband I can be for my beautiful flower. Violet loves my name for her.

JULY 14, 1979

I don't think I have ever felt so happy as I felt watching Violet walk down the church aisle yesterday. She looked angelic walking down the aisle to me. I have never seen her look more beautiful. I am still not sure I am worthy of her, but I vowed to spend every day trying. We finally made love for the first time. It's hard to fully describe what it was like to touch her finally. She is so soft, so perfect. Knowing God made her only for me. I am not sure I can ever get enough of her.

JULY 13, 1984

Today is our 5-year Anniversary! Violet gave me a framed sketch of me and my show horse. I put it over the fireplace so I could see it every day. My flower is so talented. I bought her flowers and took her out for dinner in St. Augustine. Some fancy new restaurant. The kind of place where you wear a tie. She looked so beautiful in a blue dress and high heels. How did I get so lucky? I see how others look at her, and I am thankful each day that she picked me. Over dinner, we made an important decision. We decided to start trying for a family. Not that we have been very careful, but now we are going to officially try. I want a family with Violet. A house that's loud and full of laughter. If the good Lord gives us a house full, I know we will be blessed!

OCTOBER *18, 1989*

Violet is not doing well. She tries to hide her disappointment, but I know she is hurting. Every month we pray together that this will be the month. Making love has become routine and on a schedule. Everyone is giving her advice, saying it will happen when it happens. But I am the one that sees her red-rimmed eyes as she curls up on the porch wrapped in a blanket watching another day's sunset. It has been 5 years; how much longer should we continue to try?

DECEMBER *3, 1991*

Today is a hopeful day. We visited a Fertility Clinic in the city. Over 7 years of disappointment while trying to start a family and we finally have answers. After a bunch of tests, they determined Violet still has a chance of conceiving, albeit small. Violet cried so many tears at the news. The Doctor was optimistic that with the right combination of medication she could increase her chances and should get pregnant. This is our last chance to start a family, although I told Violet I would adopt her 20 kids if that is what she wanted. She insists she wants to carry our child. So many times, I have wished the problem was me. That I could take the burden of this from her. But God had other plans. After talking through it, we are choosing to be optimistic and proceed with the medication.

. . .

MAY 22, 1992

Today is one of the best days of my life! Just when we were ready to completely give up, we found out today Violet is pregnant! What do you know, those darn drugs worked. They made her so sick to her stomach, but after realizing that the sickness seemed to only happen in the morning, she took a pregnancy test. She came racing into the barn with the positive pregnancy test in her hand, not able to wait till I came inside. I have never seen my flower happier! God is good! I cannot wait to be a daddy.

JANUARY 19, 1993

Our baby girl is here! Daisy Everleigh Wolton was born at 2:53 this morning. 6 lbs 5 oz and 20 inches long. After a long labour, she finally arrived. Violet was so brave through the delivery. My woman is strong, and I am so proud of her. Daisy is so tiny and beautiful, just like her mama, with a shock of reddish-brown hair. When I held her in my arms, I think I fell in love all over again. No one tells you what that will feel like, but it was true. Completely in love. Now I have two flowers in my bouquet. I am a truly blessed man.

JANUARY 25, 1993

I can finally take my beautiful flowers home. Seeing Violet with Ever (my nickname for my little girl) makes my heart feel so full. I feel like it may bust out of my chest. Violet was born to be a mother. She just knows exactly what Ever needs almost before she needs it. Although neither of us has gotten much sleep, we are truly happy and grateful to God for our little family.

APRIL 30, 1993

I could finally take Violet home from the hospital today. The last week has been scary. Seeing your wife collapse on the kitchen floor is enough to stop any man's heart. In the Emergency they ran some tests and found a tumour in her uterus. The tumour was the size of a baseball and they found out it was cancer. My flower had cancer growing inside her and I did not know. A few times she looked like she was in some kind of pain, but when I asked, she said it was just some cramps after childbirth or that her body was just resetting itself. "It is normal," she would tell me as she smiled and went about her day. After the surgery, the doctors said it was successful and they think they got it all. More tests will follow, but for now my flower is okay. Sadly, we cannot have any more children, but Violet says God blessed us with Daisy and we need to count our blessings. I know she is right.

MAY 19, 1994

Ever is growing up so fast! She is the prettiest little girl in Primrose and loves to spend time with me in the barn. She is fearless too, so I cannot turn my back for a second. If I turn my back even for a moment, she is in the sheep pen petting the lambs. I take her with me in the morning to do the chores to let Violet sleep. She has been so tired lately and I need to get her into the doctor soon. Since her cancer scare, we take all aches and pains seriously. Every time I suggest it, she tells me I worry too much, saying she is just tired as she has been up with Ever at night. I know my little flower is a good sleeper, so it does not make sense. Best to get her checked out.

MAY 25, 1994

The cancer is back. They did a bunch of tests and said it has spread to her bladder and liver. They say its stage four and treatments available have a very low success rate. Violet wants to go home and be in her own bed, so I took my flower home today. Her parents want her to try treatment despite the low chances of recovery, but Violet says no. "I have had a good life and want to enjoy what time I have left. I want to be home with my family," she told them. Hearing the news today, I wanted to scream, "Why? Why is cancer attacking my beautiful flower?" I just want to wrap her up and protect her, not let her feel any pain. Keep her forever with me. I know that is not God's plan, but right now, my faith is shaken.

JUNE 3, 1994

My mother-in-law has moved in to help with Ever. She wanted to take her to their house, but Violet insisted Ever stay home with us. She does not want to miss a minute of our little girl's life. Fred has been coming in each day to chore the animals, so I can spend every moment with my flower. Each day feels like a nightmare, but I try so hard to be strong for Violet. She is in so much pain, I know she is, but insists she is fine. We have medication to help her get through the pain, but as I lay next to her while she sleeps, I can feel her body tense and at times she cries out, the pain too much to bear. It is tearing me up inside. I wish I could take all her pain away, even if just for a day. Take that pain and put it on myself instead.

*J*UNE *27, 1994*

Today was a good day. Violet was in good spirits. Ever and I napped with her this afternoon, all in the big bed. After dinner, she asked if I could carry her downstairs so she could sit on her bench and watch the sunset on the porch. Ever joined us sitting beside her mom and Violet asked if I could take a picture of them. She said because they looked "Pretty as a picture". I wrapped my girls in a blanket, and we enjoyed the colors painting the prairie sky. It felt like it did when we first moved in here as newlyweds. When days were uncomplicated and simple. When life or death was not a decision. As I held my flowers and watched the sky dance in magnificent colors, I thanked God for moments like this, reminding me that I have so much to be grateful for.

CHAPTER 11

*B*en exited the barn and made his way up the path to the farmhouse. He had not seen Ever since she returned that afternoon from town. She was shaken up, he could tell. The mystery of her name and details surrounding her mother's death, a revelation that was occupying her thoughts and weighing heavily on her heart.

"Ever! Where are you, sweetheart?" he called, coming in the back door, hanging his hat on the hook.

"In Dad's office." She shouted.

Coming around the corner, he found her in Hardin's recliner, her eyes red rimmed and face wet from tears. In her hands she held an old leather journal.

"What have you been doing?" he asked, leaning down to kiss her on the head and glancing at the journal in her hands.

"I found this," she replied, passing the journal to Ben.

He opened it, reading the front cover, his eyes widening in question. "Is this his journal?"

She nodded and gave him an anguished look.

Holding out his hand, he pulled her up from her seat and wrapped his comforting arms around her. "Are you okay?"

"Yeah, I will be," she sighed, swallowing down the lump still in her throat. "Just so many secrets. I don't understand why my dad made the decisions he did. Why all the mystery? Oh, check this out..." she continued. Leaving his arms, she opened the folder; she had found earlier, still on her father's desk. Pulling out the Change of Name Application, she handed it to Ben.

Taking it from her, Ben perused the document and looked up at her in question. "But why would he go to all the trouble to change your name? And this happened after your mother's death?

She nodded, confirming his suspicions.

"That is incredibly strange." he continued his brows knitting into a frown.

"I know, right?" she agreed. "What was his motive? I guess I will never really know," she added, letting her shoulders sag in resignation.

Coming around behind her, he massaged her shoulders and she leaned back into him feeling comfort in his touch. "Thank you." She said, glancing over her shoulder at him.

Ben smiled thoughtfully then leaned down, brushing his lips to hers in a gentle kiss. "What should we do tonight?" he asked. "Perhaps we need to get out and do something fun! It's Friday after all! I know this day has been heavy for you and I want to take my sweetheart out," he confessed, turning her around to face him, wrapping his strong protective arms around her. "How about going out dancing? We could call Hayden, Bea, and some other friends too, if you like."

Ever brightened and flashed him an approving smile. Stepping away from him, she curled up her nose and she laughed. "You need a shower first, Farm Boy!"

He laughed and sniffed under his armpits. "What do you mean? I thought you liked my natural manly musk?" he asked, trying to grab her and hug her again.

She giggled squirming away from him and patted him on the chest, pushing him towards the front entrance. "Go take a shower, you big old bear!"

"Join me?" he asked, lifting his shirt over his head and waggling his eyebrows.

"We may never leave if I do," she giggled, giving him another playful shove toward the stairs.

He flashed her a sexy smile, winked and bounded up the staircase.

* * *

FINDING their way back to the "Pickled Pig", Ever could not help but feel nostalgic. It had been six weeks since that magical night they first kissed on the dance floor. The night they realized they would mean so much more to each other than an employer and employee and the weekend their relationship began. It seemed like a lifetime ago. Spending all her days and nights with Ben, their familiarity with each other, made it seem like they had been together so much longer. Her feelings were growing, and those important three words lingered between them unsaid. Sometimes when she looked into his warm blue eyes, when he smiled or glanced at her, she could see it. The love was there, but was still unspoken.

The bar was hopping and very quickly they found their friends around a booth in the corner of the bar.

"Ever!" Bea exclaimed, bounding into Ever's arms, wrapping her legs around her friend like a spider monkey.

"Dear God, Bea, you're going to knock me over!" she laughed, setting her friend down on her feet. Bea was dressed in a sparkly grey sheer button up blouse, black bra peeking through the fabric, black skinny jeans, and grey bedazzled cowboy boots. Her risqué style was something only Bea could pull off with her petite frame.

Bea waved off her friend's comment and grabbed her arm, dragging her to the bar across the room. Ever just giggled, glancing over her shoulder to Ben with a shrug as Bea led her across the dance floor to the bar. "Let's get some drinks!" Bea shouted over the loud music.

Ordering four beers for her, Ever, Ben and Hayden, Bea grabbed two of them and started back to the booth, weaving through the dense crowd. Turning with the other two beers in hand, Ever followed Bea, only to have her path blocked. A guy in his mid-twenties, about six feet tall, with longish dark brown hair and squinty brown eyes, stood in front of her. Clean shaven and hair perfectly coiffed with enough gel to choke a horse. He got into her space and leaned so close to her face she could smell the whiskey on his breath.

"Excuse me," she offered politely, trying to go around him.

He dodged in front of her, not letting her pass. "Hi

there," he said, running his hand down her arm. "I saw you at the bar." He continued looking her up and down, licking his lips. "You are so sexy."

Still not letting her through, she stopped and gave him a disgusted glare. "Can you please back off?"

"Why baby? I think you and I could have some fun together." He whispered, leaning closer to her ear; his hot rancid breath making her stomach churn. "I like hot older women, like you."

"Not interested in young punks." she spat out, her eyes blazing at him.

Annoyed by her lack of interest, he backed away, hands up in the air, his lips curled up in a snarl. "Fucking cougar!" he shouted loud enough to make heads turn on the dance floor.

Angry and still cursing, he turned around and slammed into a very large, very angry Ben.

"What did you just call my girl?" Ben asked in his deep, growly voice.

Looking up slowly, the guy swallowed down hard, his mouth agape as he took in this intimating monster of a man in front of him. 300 pounds of pure muscle. Ben towered over him, giving him a look like he was going to pound him into the ground.

"I suggest you apologize to the lady," he growled, eyes dark with fury.

The man, hesitant to turn his back from the beast of a man growling at him, turned to Ever, a look of apology and fear on his face. "I...I... am sorry," he stuttered, glancing back at Ben then running off, like a coward, disappearing into the crowd.

"Punk." Ben growled, looking after him, his face red with anger then quickly turning to face Ever, morphing from anger to concern. "Are you okay, sweetheart?"

Ever handed him his beer and wrapped her arms around his neck, looking up at her protector, then deadpanned. "I was just about to kick his ass, but thanks for the backup."

Throwing his head back in laughter, his deep rich baritone filling up the dance floor, Ben swooped her up in a big bear hug, lifting her off the ground. "I love you!" he blurted out, then stopped, giving her a wide-eyed glare, a look of uncertainty covering his admission. Realizing what he just said, he set her down on her feet, their eyes still locked on each other.

Ever's eyes shone lovingly, as she reached to him, touching his cheek with a tender caress. "I love you too, Bear."

His blue eyes twinkled at her confession as a huge smile washed over his face, making his eyes crinkle in the way she loved so much. Capturing her face in his hands, he leaned in delicately brushing his lips to hers. The emotion in the kiss was so raw and tender it made Ever's eyes well up and her heart flutter wildly.

She loved Ben, and he loved her. This big, burly beast of a man was hers and in this moment nothing else mattered.

* * *

COMING HOME LATE, tired, and a little drunk on both alcohol and love, Ben lifted Ever's feet onto his lap as they buried into the leather couch. Removing her cowboy boots one by one, he proceeded to rub her instep, eliciting a groan of pleasure from her lips. He growled in reply, waggling his eyebrows and continued his attention on her sore feet.

"How do you always seem to know just what I need?" she asked, laying her head back on the armrest with a contented sigh.

He met her gaze, his lips curling up in a sweet smile as he replied simply, "Because I love you, Ever."

Ever returned his smile, a look of joy and contentment on her face.

"Come here, sweetheart," he beckoned, patting his lap.

Obliging, she got up and climbed onto his lap, straddling him.

"I know you probably didn't come here intending to start a relationship, and never expected to fall in love with someone. I know that you have to return to Toronto in September, but right here, right now, I have you, and I want to just love you, in every way I can.", he declared, a look of reverence in his eyes.

"I want that too," she replied, looking deep into his eyes as she languidly brushed her fingers through his beard. "Now take me upstairs and make love to me, Bear."

Growling, Ben lifted her, her legs wrapped securely around his waist. Their lips crashed into each other, a tangle of tongues and promises. Promises of an uncertain but deeply desired future together.

THE SUMMER OFFICIALLY ARRIVED, and their love grew stronger with each sunset. Ever had never felt so close to anyone before and when she was not with Ben, even for a short time, she missed him. His presence gave her a sense of contentment and protection she had so long desired. Loving him was changing her, and she was both scared and exhilarated by it.

Perched on a hay bale, Ever balanced a sketchbook on her knee, pencil behind her ear. Hopeful for a break-through, she took to carrying a sketchbook around her with her. Having discovered her mother's mutual interest in art, she felt more connected to her and hoped that carrying it would bring the inspiration she needed to paint again.

Ben was busy stacking bales of hay, baseball cap on his head, shirt off, his beautiful body glistening with sweat, muscles flexing as he worked. Ever couldn't help but admire him and flashback to all the ways he could use that magnificent body to please her. Her thoughts making a tingling heat rise in her core.

Glancing over his shoulder, he gave her one of his devastating smiles. "What dirty thoughts are brewing in your head?" he asked with a chuckle as he lifted another bale onto the stack he was building.

"Me? Dirty?" she asked coquettishly, giving him a sly smile.

Laughing, he took a seat on a bale across from her, removing his hat and pulling out a bandana to wipe the sweat from his brow. Leaning back coyly, he cocked his head at her, giving her a come-hither grin.

Setting down her sketchbook and pencil, she dropped

to the floor and crawled over to him seductively. Ben's blue eyes flashed at her in approval as a growl rose deep from his throat. She ran her hands over his calves, squeezed his knees and settled her hands on his thick muscular thighs. Reaching for his belt buckle, she unfastened it.

"What are you doing?" he asked, watching her remove his belt, his breathing becoming heavy.

"Getting dirty." She replied, glancing up at him with a naughty grin as she popped the button on his work pants.

He lifted himself up so she could slide the pants down, letting them pool at his ankles. Teasingly running her hands over his thighs, she locked eyes with him as she rubbed his impressive ridge, now threatening to escape the confines of his briefs. Boldly reaching inside his briefs, she pulled out his erection, giving it a few slow and steady strokes, already glistening with the evidence of his desire. Leaning forward, she kissed the head of him and glanced up at Ben through her lashes. A deep growl of approval rose from his throat, making her smile. Taking him into her warm mouth, she began stroking and teasing him with her tongue. His salty musky arousal made her pool with desire as she licked, sucked, and swirled her tongue around him, producing primal growls of pleasure. Feeling empowered, she took him as deep as she could, allowing him to curl her hair around his fist and control her pace.

"Ever, sweetheart, I..." he panted, throwing back his head with pleasure.

She moaned around him, causing intense sensations to ricochet through his body.

"Fuck!" he shouted as his release overtook him.

Swallowing, she took every drop of his pleasure until he was left wrung out and spent. Lifting her head, she wiped her lips and gave him a wicked smile.

He met her gaze with a satisfied grin on his face. She took his face in her hands and kissed him passionately, feeling the burn of desire between them rise again. Standing and lifting her to her feet, he swooped her up in his arms, making her gasp in surprise. Gently, he laid her down on a pile of loose hay. Kicking off his boots, pants and briefs, he covered her body with his and scorched her with a burning kiss, giving her bottom lip a tug with his teeth. Lifting himself to his knees, he reached under her dress and guided her panties down her legs. She spread herself open to him, his length growing hard as steel again.

"You recover quick," she commented as he kissed her deeply and ground his hardness along the slick folds between her legs.

"Only for you sweetheart," he growled as he took her in one long delicious slide. "Tell me how you want it."

"Fast and dirty." She panted as he drew out and thrust back in. "I want you to fuck me hard."

Her permission and dirty request were all he needed. He pounded into her with long deep strokes, making her buck off the floorboards in pleasure. The sound of their sweaty hot skin connecting and guttural cries echoing in the loft. Driven insane with their pleasure they came tumbling together into ecstasy.

Afterwards they lay there, hot and sticky with sweat in the pile of hay, basking in their post sex haze. "Well, that was hot!" she suddenly exclaimed, turning to him. "A literal roll in the hay!"

Ben laughed huskily and kissed her affectionately. "I don't even want to think about all the places I have hay right now!" he commented, giving her an amused sideways smile.

"A not so sexy side effect of amorous farm activities." she deadpanned.

Ben let out a huge deep laugh, pulling her into him, the sounds of their laughter echoing through the entire barn.

CHAPTER 12

Waking from a vivid dream, Ever took a moment to take in her surroundings. She was in her bed, Ben snoring steadily beside her, his large body a wall of warmth. Sitting up, she swung her legs out of the bed and padded to the bathroom. Taking in her reflection in the mirror, she splashed water on her face and wiped her eyes. Her dream felt so real, it was hard to shake. Flashing back to the reverie of her dream she saw her mother's silhouette in the middle of a wheat field. The sun just peeking over the horizon. She looked angelic, glowing, her silhouette a vision as Ever walked slowly towards her. When she reached her mother, she smiled and took Ever's hands in hers. Her hazel eyes were bright with knowing she said. *"You already have all that you need."* Then turned and glided away through the field, disappearing into the horizon.

Ever shook her head, trying to break out of her trance. She'd had similar dreams to this in the past. Every time in a wheat field, someone stands off in the distance. The feeling of familiarity, strong but no face visible. This dream had been part of her existence for as long as she could remember. It reoccurred mostly in the summer, and she was always perplexed by what it meant. She now understood. Her mother was visiting her, letting her know she was with her.

In this dream however, she spoke, giving her a message. She could not shake her words *"You already have all that you need." What did that mean?* Rubbing her hands over her face, she made her way back down the hallway, glancing to her left at the large window framing the upstairs overhang that looked down on the front yard. The sun was rising, and flecks of gold flickered over the wheatfield, making them look like spun gold.

"You already have everything you need", her mother's voice echoed in her head.

Entranced, Ever made her way down the stairs and out the front door, taking in the beginnings of a beautiful prairie sunrise. Quickly going back inside, she grabbed her canvas and positioned it on the porch, giving her the best view of the emerging sky, then rushed back into the house to grab paints, a palette, and brushes. Once her palette was prepared, she looked to the sky, picked up the brush with shaking hands and started to paint.

* * *

BEN WOKE WITH A STARTLE, his hand automatically feeling the empty space next to him. The sweet smell of Ever lingered on her pillow. He inhaled deeply. Sitting up, he wiped the sleep from his eyes and looked at the bedside clock. 5:30 a.m.

"Ever?" he called out. No answer. *That's not like her to be up so early.* Getting out of bed, he pulled on a pair of jeans and made his way down the staircase, glancing in the living room, only to spot her on the front porch through the picture window. Quietly making his way out onto the porch, he saw she had her easel set up, was holding a paintbrush, and looking towards the sky. Taking a seat on the bench, he looked out at the magnificent sunrise unfolding before him. The sky was clear, not a cloud to be seen and glimmers of gold kissed the horizon, making the wheat of the neighbour's field sparkle like glitter. As the sun rose, the layer of gold reflected on the blue sky made the sky look like something out of a dream.

"It's beautiful." he mused, looking at Ever.

She smiled in agreement, her eyes transfixed on her canvas and the prairie sky. Her brush moved in steady strokes across the canvas, capturing the scene in front of them. They stayed there together for a while, in silence. The only sound was her brush strokes and a light breeze swaying the golden wheat in the field. It was peaceful. A morning that made you feel closer to God.

He looked to Ever feeling overwhelmed by his feelings for her as she painted, barefoot, only covered by a thin blue chemise nightgown, her body silhouetted by the emerging light. Her flawless skin glowed and her wild from sleep reddish-brown hair shimmered like a halo around her head. As he watched her, completely enraptured by her beauty and overcome with emotions, he realised he had never seen anyone more beautiful, and he had never loved anyone more.

* * *

AFTER THE MORNING on the porch, it was like a dam had broken. Inspiration flowing like a stream through her days. Ever painted canvas after canvas. Beautiful, surreal images captured around the farm. Images of the sky, flowers, the fields, the barn, and animals. Even images of Ben. One morning, as he stood at the corner of the front porch, coffee in hand, gazing out over the front lawn. The striking line of his body begged to be painted, so he indulged her as she captured the moment. "The Protector" she called the painting. It seemed to fit.

She was falling deeper in love with Ben every day and knowing that their days together were numbered was a reality she knew she could no longer ignore. *What if I move back to Prairie Sky?* she asked herself. *Would I be giving up on my dreams?* These questions weighed heavily on her, as did the future of the farm. The more she thought about Prairie Sky Acres, the answer as to its fate became crystal clear.

* * *

"NICE TO SEE YOU AGAIN, EVER!" Mr. Estes greeted her. "I assume since you are here, you have made a decision on the farm."

"I have."

Mr. Estes, her father's long-time friend and lawyer,

gestured for her to take a seat. Taking a seat across from him she put her hands in her lap and looked up to him. "I have decided not to sell."

"Oh!" he exclaimed in surprise. "What would you like to do, then?"

"If it is possible, I would like to give the farm to Ben Hastings. Ben has been a part of the farm for seven years and I know he loved and respected my father." She explained. "Prairie Sky Acres is just as much a part of me as it is a part of him."

"So, you will be returning to Toronto?" he inquired, eyebrows raised in curiosity.

"I still plan to, yes. I'll go back in 5 weeks." She replied. "Ben can step in as owner without any hiccup in the farm business. He already manages everything, so the transition should be simple."

Mr. Estes nodded his head and smiled at Ever. "I think your father would have approved of your decision. Hardin had a lot of respect for Ben too and often told me he thought of him as a son."

"I think so too," she mused. "Also, no money is exchanging hands. This is a gift, plain and simple. A gift I am freely giving." She explained.

"Wow, okay! As the sole beneficiary of your father's estate, we have just recently completed a transfer of ownership to your name, so you and Ben will have to sign a Gift of Ownership."

"Perfect." She replied as she stood. "Let me know when we can come in to sign the paperwork."

"I will.", he replied.

"One more thing.", she turned to face him again.

Mr. Estes nodded.

"Can this be done by the beginning of September, preferably before the Labour Day Weekend?" She asked.

"Absolutely."

* * *

THE BELL of the front door chimed, and Ben looked around the Hastings Hardware Store, spotting Hayden at the back of the store helping a customer. Waiting at the front, Hayden spotted him and gave him a wave.

"Hey Bro, be right with you!"

Hayden finished up with the customer and helped ring up the customer's order. As the customer exited the store, Hayden settled his gaze on his brother as he leaned on the front counter. "What's up Ben? You look like you have a lot going through your head."

"I do." Ben replied simply.

Hayden rolled his eyes at his brother's lack of details and rounded the counter to stand beside him. "Does this have to do with Ever leaving in what, four weeks?" he asked, an eyebrow raised in question.

Ben met his brother's gaze and nodded, looking down at his boots. "I really don't want her to go."

"So, tell her." Hayden whispered as he nodded, acknowledging two customers entering the store.

"I can't do that Hayden." Ben said, a look of defeat on his face. "Her life is in Toronto; her dream is wrapped into that city. I simply cannot ask that of her."

Putting his hand on his brother's shoulder in consolation, he gave it a squeeze. "Have you ever thought that maybe, you are now part of her dream?" he asked. "You love her, right?"

Ben looked at his brother and nodded.

"Then fight for her, Ben. Show her why she should stay."

* * *

PUTTING DOWN HER PAINTBRUSH, Ever grabbed her phone that was buzzing beside her and smiled, recognizing the number. "Hello Whitney!"

Whitney Faris was her art agent whom she met shortly after completing her art education. A native Torontonian, Whitney was beautiful, sharp witted and fun. She loved art as much as Ever and had been with her through every step of her art career, always championing for her and helping her make important connections. She had also become one of her best friends and Ever thought of her more as an older sister than her agent.

"Ever, I have missed you!

"I have missed you too!" Ever replied.

"I got your text and the pictures of your latest work. They are simply gorgeous! Your best work yet." Whitney appraised. "I showed your new paintings to the Art Director at the gallery you last showed at, and she is very interested in doing an exhibit of your new work."

"Wow, that is amazing!"

"It is! This is exactly what you need right now to get your work out there again! Out of curiosity, what has caused this breakthrough?" she inquired with genuine interest.

"So many things. The past three months have been some of the best of my life." Ever replied, nestling herself into the living room couch. "Returning to the farm has flooded me with memories, has answered so many unknown questions about my mother and the biggest surprise of all, has brought Ben into my life."

"Ben?" Whitney asked the pitch of her voice, raising a few octaves. "Is he the inspiration behind "The Protector?"

"He is. I love him, Whitney.", she confessed.

"Oh Ever, I am so incredibly happy for you!" she gushed with the sincerity of a true friend. "Are you still planning to return to Toronto?"

"Yes, that still is the plan."

"Oh, okay! Selfishly, I am happy you are coming back. But how is that going to work?" Whitney questioned.

"We have discussed it briefly, but honestly, I'm not 100% sure.", she sighed. "Do long-distance relationships even work?"

"I don't know Ever. But I know you and when you want something, you don't give up."

Ever contemplated her words. *Were they going to be able to make a long-distance relationship work?* She didn't know, but she knew she had to try. Her love for Ben was too strong to simply give up. She couldn't imagine him not being in her future.

Breaking the silence, Whitney exclaimed. "Enjoy that hunky man of yours and I expect pictures!"

"Just texted you one.", Ever replied with a giggle, obliging her friend's request.

"Yes, let's see here…. Oh, dear Lord, Ever, he is…. Wow, just wow!"

"He has a brother, Whitney!" Ever shared teasingly.

"Don't tempt me," she replied. "One more thing before I go. Can you promise me something?"

"What?"

"You will enjoy the rest of your time there. Every moment. You deserve so much happiness, my friend."

Ever smiled at Whitney's request. Ben made her happy. Happier than she had ever been. She decided right then to take her friend's advice. Over the next four weeks, she was going to put aside their impending goodbyes and spend every moment she could, wrapped in his arms.

CHAPTER 13

On the August long weekend, they took a little road trip. Ben asked Hayden to check in on the animals, so they had three full days together. Deciding to go camping, they packed up Ben's truck with all their supplies, food, and coolers.

"Where exactly are you taking me?" she asked as they pulled onto the highway heading southeast.

Ben winked at Ever and laughed. "Just wait, so impatient! This is a place I like to fish sometimes, a little off the beaten path."

"So, it's by the water? A lake, a river?"

"Yes," he replied with an eyebrow raised. "I hope you brought your swimsuit."

"I did."

"A bikini?" he growled in question, giving her a wicked grin.

Grinning back, she gave him a wink and replied, "Perhaps."

* * *

After a two-hour drive, they finally arrived at their destination. Turning down a dirt path, tall evergreens lined the road as they drove deep into a secluded area of bush. Suddenly, a clearing appeared next to a small lake. On one side of the lake, a narrow beach lined the bank and just down from the beach, a dock jutted out onto the lake, perfect for fishing.

Getting out of the truck, Ever walked down to the end of the dock, taking in the scene in front of them. Tall evergreens surrounded the lake, the water shimmered in the sun as it rippled from the breeze. The water was clean and clear, just right for swimming. She couldn't think of a more perfect place for them to escape to for their weekend together. A private and unexpected oasis.

Ben started to unload their supplies and Ever wrapped her arms around his back in a reverse hug. "I love this place."

Turning himself around, he wrapped his arms around her and lifted her up in his arms, planting a sweet kiss on her lips. "I knew you would," he replied, swinging her around, a joyful giggle escaping her mouth.

Putting her down on her feet, he gave her another chaste kiss as they continued unloading the truck and started setting up the tent together. Once their camp was set up, Ben started on a fire with some firewood he brought from the farm. Setting up the lawn chairs around the fire, Ever took a seat and watched him as he stoked the fire with a long stick. The haze of early evening was emerging, and it gave the clearing a feeling of peaceful tranquility. Her recent creative awakening made her think of the shadows reflecting on the water and how she would paint them.

Ben glanced over at Ever and moved his chair right next to hers. "What are you thinking, sweetheart?"

"About how I would paint those reflections on the water." She grinned at him. "I just see color, shade, contrast everywhere."

Ben reached for her hand and intertwined his fingers with hers. "Ever, I am so happy you are painting again."

She smiled in reflection. "It feels good. I feel like a faucet you cannot turn off. I feel like I did when I left Prairie Sky for Toronto. Like my creativity is over-flowing."

Ben turned to stare at the fire, both falling into quiet contemplation. "Can I ask you something?" he asked, breaking their reverie.

"Anything."

"I know we have never really discussed it and I never wanted to ask you because I didn't want to bring up anything painful, but…"

"You want to know why my dad and I had not spoken for so long?"

He nodded, stoking their fire causing golden embers to rise into the sky.

Ever swallowed, an emotional tightness forming in her throat. Thinking back to the day that changed her life forever was difficult. A day that was burnt into her brain and branded on her heart. She sighed as she shared her story.

"My dad was always very protective." she began

entranced by the fire. "He always wanted what was best for me, or at least what he thought was best for me. My senior year of high school, the Counsellor encouraged me to apply to several art schools as by then it was very clear art was my passion and the teachers thought I had a genuine talent. My dad would never really acknowledge that passion and encouraged me to consider teaching or business, something that would keep me close to Primrose and close to him. He also would never attend any of my school art shows and would say to me, *'Art will not pay the bills.'* She looked at Ben with sadness in her eyes. "I was not accepted right away into any of the art schools, so after graduation I worked for my dad, helped with bookkeeping and took a job at the Eazy, trying to figure out what to do next".

Ben nodded, taking in her story, encouraging her to continue.

"Well, one year after graduation, I continued to paint whenever I had a chance and reapplied to my number one choice of schools, Toronto School of Art. Early that following winter, I received a letter of acceptance telling me there was a spot for me in spring."

"Amazing." he acknowledged, looking at her with a smile.

"I thought so, but I was scared to share it with dad as I was sure he would discourage me from going. So, I kept it from him for a few months, until I could figure out the details and finally mustered up enough courage to tell him."

Ben met her gaze and squeezed her hand.

"He was in his barn office, and I sort of blurted it out,

not very eloquently in fact, and showed him the letter of acceptance. His response was an immediate 'No'. After that, it was all a bit of a blur. I was upset, obviously, and we didn't talk much for several days. It was February at the time and the start of Art School was about three months away. The tension being too much to bear, I asked Bea if I could stay at her house temporarily until he calmed down or finally decided to accept my decision." she said with a look of regret on her face. "In retrospect, I knew it was a bad idea, but I was so determined and wanted my independence so fiercely that I felt doing something drastic would get his attention and make him realize how unreasonable he was being. So, I wrote him a note telling him my plans and that if he wanted to talk to me again, I would be at Bea's. I packed my things and loaded my car, internally praying he would not notice me, as I didn't want a confrontation. I was not that lucky. Coming in from the barn, he caught me carrying the last of my bags down the stairs."

"He must have been shocked." Ben offered.

"I think he was. He just looked at me with a combination of anger and hurt. I have never seen him look so incredibly hurt. He told me 'If you think this place is not good enough for you, leave, go and don't even think of coming back.' So, I left."

Ben leaned forward and rubbed his hand over his beard, then turned to meet Ever's regretful gaze. "So that was the last time you saw him?"

"Yes."

Both sat there for a few minutes, staring into the fire. "I am so sorry Ever."

Giving him a grateful look, she squeezed his hand. "Honestly, I never thought it would be the last time I would see him. I honestly thought if I left, spent a few weeks with Bea he would calm down, accept that I needed to follow my dreams and would finally be happy for me. After a month, I realized that was not going to happen. So, I left for Toronto early, driving three days till I got there, in the middle of winter no less."

"What did you do when you got there? Did you have a place to stay?" he asked.

"No, I had nothing, just my things in the back of my car. I had saved a significant amount of money, so I rented a long-term hotel room by the airport and started hunting for an apartment. Of course, everything was incredibly expensive, but finally I found a sublet on a loft apartment that was reasonable enough. I still have that apartment. It is small but is in a great area and has fantastic lighting for painting."

"Wow, so you were completely on your own?" he asked.

"Yes, for a few months. My building manager and neighbours were nice and once I started school, I met some new friends. It was a very difficult, lonely time for me. A lot of emotions, which I think benefited my painting. It became my therapy in a way."

"I can see that," he mused. "So, did your father ever reach out to you?"

"Not that I know of. I reached out to him a few times over the years. First time I sent him an invitation to my first gallery showing and then again, I sent him a letter telling him I missed him. I never got anything in return."

Ben sat back in his chair and stared at the fire. The shadows deepened as the sun set behind the trees. "Do you think maybe he felt abandoned?" he asked, looking into her eyes. "I mean your mom passed away and from what you told me about his journal, he took her passing very hard."

"I think so. Finding my dad's journal really helped to make more sense out of his reaction. I think he was just scared of losing me, after losing so much in the past." She replied, a look of comprehension on her face. "But why shut me out completely? Why tell me to leave and not come back? I guess I will never know." She resolved, looking into the fire. *I guess I will never know.*

THE NEXT MORNING Ben woke early, the sound of birds chirping and the light summer breeze swaying the trees. Ever was sound asleep next to him. Her wavy hair splayed out above her. She looked peaceful and her body was so gloriously warm next to him. Pulling her even closer into the contours of his body, he sighed. *What am I going to do without her?* In such a short time, she had become everything to him. His days revolved around when he would see her, hold her, and make love to her next. The thought of not seeing her every day made his throat tight and heart ache. *What am I going to do?*

Stirring from sleep, Ever opened her eyes drowsily. Burrowing his scruff into her neck, he softly kissed her cheek, then her neck, making goosebumps appear on her skin. "Good morning, Sweetheart. How did you sleep?"

"Like a baby." She sighed with a smile as she pressed her bottom against him, arousing him to life. "Couldn't get a larger sleeping bag?" she joked regarding the tight confines of their extra-large sleeping bag.

"You mean you don't want to be this close to me?" he teased gently nipping her ear with his teeth then giving it a suck, making her writhe and giggle with delight.

Shimmying herself to face him, she reached up and ran her fingers through his beard and up to his head, tugging playfully at his messy hair.

"God, I love that."

"What, me pulling your hair?" she asked, giving it another tug.

Contentedly, he smiled and closed his eyes. "No, sweetheart. I love it when you touch me. I love you so much Ever." His blue eyes opened, reflecting his fears and sadness at their impending goodbyes.

"Oh, Bear, I love you too. You look so sad. What's wrong?"

Ben met her gaze, unshed tears making his blue eyes glisten. She knew at that instant what was bothering him.

"Bear, I don't know what the future has in store for us," she reassured, lovingly caressing his cheek. "Let's live in the moment. Right here, right now. That is all I can promise."

Ever unzipped the sleeping bag, allowing them to move more freely. She kissed him passionately, her tongue gliding with his. Swinging her legs over him, she rested her centre over his hardness. "Make love to me, Ben."

Looking up at this gorgeous woman on top of him,

this woman he loved so much, he lifted her nightgown over her head, revealing her beautiful breasts peaked and awaiting his touch. She leaned over him, allowing him to take one in his mouth. Licking and sucking, he worshipped them, caressing her milky soft skin. Running his hands down her naked back, he admired the contours he had grown so familiar with over the past months. There was nothing more beautiful he thought than Ever naked, vulnerable, and trusting in front of him. Reaching down, he slid down his sleep pants and moved aside her panties, feeling her wetness soak his fingers. She was ready for him. Rising, Ever let him position himself at her entrance and she sank down his hard length, taking every inch he had. She moaned, making him throb and thicken inside her. She was so warm, so tight, so perfect.

"Look at me, sweetheart," he murmured.

Ever's eyes opened, her lustful gaze melting him.

"I want to see you when we make love. I want to know you are here with me."

Her gaze transfixed on him, she moved. Rising and falling on him in delicious strokes, moving slow and deliberate. Their breaths, pants, and moans, in sync with each other. Their bodies moved as one, feeling every pang of desire, promise and hope as they savored their connection in both body and soul. They climbed the mountain together, slowly and steadily, each other's names on their lips as they reached the summit together. Feeling lost in their feelings and uncertain if that was going to be enough.

* * *

After a quick breakfast, Ever took advantage of the warm weather and hopefully warm lake. Slipping into her bikini and a pair of cut-offs she sauntered out of the tent swaying her hips seductively. Ben lifted his sunglasses, eyebrows raised, as she slowly slithered over to him. Rounding his shoulders, she trailed her fingertips over his muscles, watching them twitch under her touch. Coming around to face him again, she reached for his beard and pulled him in for a scorching kiss.

Ben growled from behind his sunglasses.

She winked wickedly as she skipped down to their little private beach.

Ever lay on the beach all afternoon, sketchbook in hand, capturing their beautiful surroundings. Ben fished on the dock, and she couldn't help but capture his image. A true country boy in his element. Enjoying the simple pleasures of a quiet afternoon in the middle of nowhere.

"Man, it's getting hot. Is it safe to swim here?" she asked. "No sharks?"

"No, sweetheart!" Ben laughed. "The water is clean, at least as clean as a lake gets. Just watch your feet as the edge of the beach is a little rocky," he warned.

"Ben, you forget I am originally a farm girl." She stood, hands on her hips. "As a kid, I never had shoes on! I literally would run on the gravel road barefoot."

"Fair enough" he held up his hands.

She removed her shorts, revealing a tiny bikini bottom that made Ben whistle at her and woot out loud in appreciation.

"Dirty old man!" she shouted as she made it across the rocky bank and waded into the lake.

Putting down his fishing rod, Ben replied, feigning insult, "Who are you calling old?"

"You!" she giggled, the water now to her waist.

"I'll show you." he laughed, slipping off his swim trunks and standing on the dock buck naked.

Ever laughed at the sight of him. Standing there at the end of the dock, sexy, ripped muscles, glowing tanned chest and torso, impressive dangling manhood and snow-white ass. Flexing his biceps, he turned and gave his tight backside a little wiggle for her.

"Nice ass, farm boy!" she teased, referring to the unfortunate hazard of his job.

"Glad you like it!" he replied, waggling his eyebrows. "Got room for me in that lake?"

"I think so." she giggled as he jumped in after her, creating a huge splash and soaking her face and hair.

She giggled and splashed him back, both starting a war of water. Their laughs echoing over the lake. Completely drenched, Ben caught Ever by the waist, not allowing her to struggle free.

"Bear!" she squealed as he growled in her ear. "Okay, okay, I surrender."

He kissed her neck and let her go, pushing his big body into the middle of the lake. Ever swam up to the dock, turned and caught his gaze on her. Reaching around her back, she untied her bikini top and reached down to shimmy out of her bottoms, putting them both on the dock.

Ben transfixed on her, took in her breasts bobbing on the surface of the water with appreciation as she waded back to him. Wrapping her arms around his neck, she pulled him in for a long passionate kiss. He smoothed her wet hair from her face and ran his hands down her back to her behind, lifting her to wrap her legs around his waist. "You are so incredibly beautiful."

She smiled happily at him and kissed him again softly, meeting his blue gaze. "And you are so handsome." She complimented back as she ran her hands through his wet hair, giving it a tug. "We would have super cute babies!" Ever laughed, releasing her grip on him, and playfully pushing him away from her with her feet.

"Babies?" he questioned playfully. "Are you thinking about babies now? Why Ms. Wolton, I think you need to put a ring on it first," he joked, waving his hand in the air and bringing it down with a splash.

Ever turned away laughing, wiping the water from her face. "Do you want marriage and a family someday?" she asked him curiously, paddling closer to him.

"Of course," he replied, swimming up to her and wrapping her around him again. "And you?"

"You know, I have never given it much thought until recently." she mused as she met his eyes.

"Really?" he asked, his mouth lifting into a happy grin.

"Really." she smiled back. "I mean, I am 30, not super experienced with relationships, before you, of course."

He nodded, acknowledging their mutual lack of experience.

"So, I kind of thought maybe marriage, and a family weren't something meant for me. But now, here with you. I think it would be nice," she reflected lovingly, meeting his eyes.

"I think it would be amazing," he added, leaning into her for a sweet kiss.

That night they made love under the stars, both understanding that their futures, however uncertain, belonged to each other.

CHAPTER 14

The next two weeks sped by faster than Ever wanted. Knowing her time at Prairie Sky was coming to its inevitable end, Ever worked tirelessly to pack up her father's office and belongings. Most of the general farm business was done from the barn office, while the paperwork stored in his home office was personal. Good on his word, Ben joined her as she went through the bookshelves, boxing up things to give away and items she wanted to take with her.

"Wow, your dad has a lot of livestock magazines!" Ben mused as he sat at her father's desk and paged through one.

Ever laughed in agreement. "Dad was never much for throwing things away."

Pulling down several books, she ran her hands over the westerns her father loved so much. Jean M. Auel, Louis L'Amour & Zane Grey Classics all worn and read countless times. Putting them into a KEEP box, she noticed another classic on the shelf. *Catcher in the Rye.*

Running her hand over the cover, she took in the laminate of a library or schoolbook. Opening the front cover, she saw the familiar stamp of PRIMROSE HIGH SCHOOL. Smiling remembering her father's journal, she hugged it to her chest and put it in her keep box. Ben sifted through some folders, putting aside anything that looked important, then lifted a file box onto the desk to go through it next. He stopped as he lifted the lid of the box.

Looking over his shoulder, her eyes widened. The box was full of photos. Photos of her mother. Photos of her. Photos she had never seen. Photos, it appeared, her father had hidden away. Ever put her hand over her mouth in disbelief. "Ben, let's go through these in the living room."

Ben nodded and grabbed the box, following her to the couch as she cleared the coffee table and took a seat. He sat down next to her and pulled out a bunch of the photos, handing them to her one by one. Faded pictures of her parents when they were young, pictures of their wedding, photos of camping and fishing trips, arms around family and friends, pictures together on horseback. So many photos showing the mystery life of her parents that she was never told of. Sifting through the box, Ben found a bunch of Ever. Handing one to her, she took in a photo of her mother, her reddish-brown hair long and braided, tendrils of wispy hairs framing her face. Her eyes were bright, cheeks rosy, and smile was wide. She was so beautiful. In her arms was a pink bundle, the face of a sleeping baby barely visible in the picture. Looking at the back, it said - *My Flowers, my loves – January 19, 1993.*

"This is the day I was born," she commented, handing the picture to Ben.

He took the picture in with a smile. "Your Mom was beautiful."

Ever nodded and took back the picture, giving it another look before setting it on the pile. Leaning back on the couch, she closed her eyes and sighed.

"Are you okay?" he asked, putting his hand on her thigh as he snuggled in next to her.

She slowly opened her eyes and turned to face him with a reassuring smile. "I will be fine. Seeing that picture, she looks just like she does in my dreams."

Ben's eyes widened as he sat up and turned to face her. "You dream about her?"

She nodded. "I've had a recurring dream since I was a child. My mother is standing in a wheat field, and I walk up to her slowly. Not until recently has her face been visible. That is the face I see now." She said pointing to the picture.

"Does she talk to you?" he asked curiously, reaching for her hand.

"Not until recently." She replied. "She always says the same thing - you already have all you need."

Pulling her onto his lap, she gazed at him warmly. "I don't know exactly what she means, but the night before I started painting again, she finally became visible in my dreams."

Ben's eyes crinkled in a wistful grin. "I don't know either, but perhaps she wanted to reassure you. Tell you to look within and around you. That even though you thought something was broken or wrong with you because you were unable to paint, she was saying nothing was missing all along. At least that's how I read her words."

She caressed his cheek and brushed her lips to his softly. "Ben Hastings, you are a wise man."

"I try." he winked, wrapping her in a warm embrace.

They sat there together for a few minutes, Ever relishing the feel of his arms around her, a constant support and comfort.

Turning to the fireplace, Ever looked up to the sketch above the hearth. "Did I tell you my mother drew that?"

His eyes followed hers and took in the beautiful sketch displayed there. "Really? I have always loved that picture. Are you taking it with you?"

"No," Ever smiled, "my mother put there it and that's where it should stay."

"But what if the new tenants or owners remove it?" he asked, genuinely concerned with her choice.

"Trust me, they won't."

BEN FINISHED up taking in a feed delivery and spotted Ever making her way down the path to the barn. *She looks so gorgeous.* Her hair swept up in a clip with tendrils escaping, framing her face. She was dressed comfortably in a soft pink cotton sundress, a denim jacket, and leather sandals.

"You look pretty," he mused, taking her in with appreciation.

"Thank you." She curtsied, making him laugh. "Bear, is

it possible to go into town this afternoon? I would like you to come with me."

"Sure, is everything okay?" he asked, his eyebrows raised in concern.

She reached up to run her fingers through his dusty beard. "Yes, Bear. Are you almost done here?"

"Yes, just going to lock up and come inside to clean up," he replied. "Where are we going?"

She smiled and reached up to kiss him softly. "You will find out."

* * *

SHOWERED AND DRESSED, Ben and Ever drove into Primrose, Ever directing him to the law office of ESTES & PARKER.

"Do you have an appointment?" he questioned. "I can stay here in the truck and wait for you."

"We have an appointment." She informed him as she opened the door and hopped out of the truck.

Confused, Ben followed her into the building and watched as she told the receptionist they were there to see Mr. Estes, who he knew was Hardin's lawyer.

Mr. Estes came out of his office and greeted them. "Ever. Ben. So glad you could come in!"

Ben shook his hand and followed Ever into his office, taking a seat across from the desk. Ever sensed his confusion, took his hand, and gave it a squeeze of reassurance.

"So, Ben, you are probably wondering why you're here with Ever and I." offered Mr. Estes.

"Yes." he replied, confusion overtaking his expression as he looked from Mr. Estes to Ever and back.

"Ever has decided on the future of the farm and has given Prairie Sky to you."

Ben felt his throat constrict and his stomach do a flip flop. *Had he heard him correctly?* "Excuse me?" he asked, eyes wide with shock.

"Ben, I know my dad would want you to have the farm. He knew how much you loved it and treated it like you would your own. You were not just his farm hand; you were like a son to him. He saw the future of our family farm in you."

Ben leaned back in his chair, shock clear on his face, and wiped his hand over his beard in disbelief. His eyes welled up with tears.

Ever slipped out of her seat, crouched down in front of him, and caught his gaze. "Bear. I want this for you. I don't need anything, no money. Nothing. I'm okay. I just want you to have your farm. I want you to have your dream."

He closed his eyes, feeling overwhelmed by this generous life changing gift he was being given. Prairie Sky was everything he always dreamt of owning someday and now the woman he loved, his girlfriend, his future, if she was willing, was gifting him the Wolton family farm. A place her father fought to keep through blinding grief and insurmountable challenges. She wanted him to carry their legacy.

Opening his eyes, a single tear rolled down his cheek and Ever caught it as she caressed the side of his face. "Will you accept this gift from me?" she asked, her hazel eyes searching his.

Ben met her gaze, so full of love and sincerity. In her eyes he saw hope, resolution and an excruciatingly beautiful kindness that made his throat tighten with emotion. "Are you sure?" he questioned, his deep voice cracking.

"I have never been more sure. Daddy would have wanted you to have it."

"I agree." confirmed Mr. Estes. "Hardin had a deep respect for you, Ben."

Ben looked at Mr. Estes and back to Ever's loving eyes. "I accept," he agreed as he wiped another tear away, stood and pulled Ever up to her feet. Taking her into his arms, he hugged her tightly with all the gratitude he could give her. "Thank you," he whispered.

SITTING on the front porch steps, a morning coffee in hand, Ever looked out over the front lawn of Prairie Sky. The summer was almost over, and she could not imagine spending her mornings any other way. Watching the sun come up over the horizon, a glowing orb slowly breaching the skyline, reflecting on the gold of the wheat fields across the way. *How can I leave all this beauty behind? What if I stayed?* The internal struggle made her head spin and heart ache.

Last night she dreamt about her mother again. The dream started as it always did. Walking towards her in the wheat field, her angelic figure taking her hands. This time she looked Ever in the eyes, smiled, and spoke. *"You know where you belong. I am close if you need me."* Her words were so clear and reassuring. She woke up feeling an immense peace.

Ben came around the house, already in his work clothes, and made his way down the walkway to the house. Climbing the stairs, he joined her on the porch and looked out over the emerging sky. Leaning into him, Ever relished the warmth of his presence next to her. She wanted him next to her always, every day. She smiled up at him and he met her eyes, his smile bright and wistful. Leaning down, he gently brushed his lips to hers so full of love and devotion. His arm came around her as she melted into his side, both watching the sky unfold before them. These quiet moments like this was one thing she loved about Ben. How he could just be still with her.

"Ben?" she asked, breaking their reverie.

"Yes, sweetheart?"

"Can we go for a ride today? Could you saddle up my dad's horse for me?" she asked. "I don't have much time left and I haven't had a chance to ride yet."

"Sure!" he replied excitedly. "I didn't know that was something you would want to do. I would love to go for a ride today. It's Sunday and not much going on, so let's pack a picnic and saddle up the horses."

"Awesome! But let's just sit here a bit longer." She said, looking towards the awakening sky. "It's just too beautiful to miss."

He leaned his head onto hers as they shared the sunrise together.

Ever strapped on the backpack she'd loaded with sandwiches, drinks, and snacks, then rubbed the soft nuzzle of her father's Arabian gelding.

"Do you need my help to get on?" Ben asked, patting his Arabian chestnut mare.

"No, I got this," she replied, putting her boot into the stirrup and mounting her horse like a pro. "This isn't my first rodeo, Cowboy." she winked.

Ben laughed and mounted his horse, adjusting the reins in his hands. "Where were you thinking we should ride?"

"Let's ride down the road a bit and to that cluster of trees off in the distance, in the middle of that field," she suggested, pointing in the general direction, and stepping her horse in line with his. "Dad and I would ride out there all the time. He always said it was one of his favorite spots."

"Sounds great!" Ben agreed, as they rode down the driveway and west down the gravel road.

They rode together talking, and Ever shared stories of the trail rides she and her father used to take. Her father loved all things horses, was a cowboy through and through and she loved the quality time they spent together, just the two of them, on horseback. It was something they mutually enjoyed and bonded them even when they disagreed or butted heads on other matters. *What would I give to have one last ride with my dad?* The happy memories washed over her, and she smiled.

"You look so deep in thought." Ben observed riding up beside her.

"Just thinking about how much I loved riding with my

dad. It was something that always connected us. I miss him so much. I feel like he is here with us." she smiled in reflection.

Ben smiled back knowingly. "I have no doubt he is."

They rode two miles down the road and across the neighbor's field to the trees. The cluster was about a quarter mile in diameter and was a well-known refuge for wildlife. Deer, foxes, rabbits and even a moose were once spotted amongst these trees. Breaching the treeline, it was like going into a wooded wonderland so different from the wide-open prairie expanse.

"This is incredible!" Ben exclaimed as they rode amongst the trees.

Ever offered him a grin, remembering how much she loved this secret place she and her father escaped to.

A red fox darted out in front of them a few paces and disappeared behind a pile of large rocks. She glanced at Ben to see if he saw it, too. He was smiling ear to ear, enjoying every moment in this secluded place.

"Should we find a place to settle in for lunch?" she asked. "If I remember correctly, there is a little pond close to the middle where we can let the horses drink too. Follow me."

She led them to the middle of the wooded area and a small body of water appeared. Dismounting their horses, they led them to the water, allowing them to take a deep drink before tethering them to a tree and finding a place to sit on the large rocks at the side of the pond.

"I forgot how quiet it is here." Ever mused as she removed the contents of her backpack.

"You said this was your dad's favorite place to ride?"

"Yeah! We would sometimes come here together, but mostly he came here on his own. I think he enjoyed the quiet and needed a place to escape at times," she reflected. "Now when I think back, when he would saddle his horse and ride off, he always came back happier."

"I could see that. Your father was a solitary man." Ben added. "He was social enough, but you could tell that he loved his time alone."

She nodded in agreement.

"Well, if you're going to be alone, this is as good a place as any," he continued as he looked around marveling at their surroundings.

"It's funny, though, whenever he came back and I asked him where he was, he would always say, 'Just paying her a visit.'"

Ben's eyebrows went up. "Do you think he came here to talk to your mom?"

"Oh, probably!" she answered. "When I was younger, I always thought he was referring to this place as 'her', but now, knowing what I know, I think he probably went here to visit my mom."

Ben looked out over the pond, reflecting on her words. "I like that."

"Me too." She replied, intertwining her hand in his.

They enjoyed their lunch and took a walk around the pond and explore a few of the trails. A short trail wound through the trees and led to a cluster of rocks that looked like they were piled strategically rather than in a natural formation.

"What's that?" Ben asked as they approached the pile of rocks. A wooden cross came into view and Ever looked at him with a look of realization on her face. Approaching the cross, she noticed it was intricately carved with flowers and a name. Ever put her hand to her mouth and whispered. "Violet."

* * *

THEY SAT THERE next to her mother's grave for a long time, Ben's arms around Ever as she cried. Coming across the grave of her mother, a mother she never knew, was a lot to take in. She cried not only for her mother but for her father, too. Their beautiful love story and his lifelong devotion to her. It was tragic, but magical.

"Your father picked a beautiful place for her to rest," Ben whispered in her ear.

She smiled and wiped at the tears rolling down her cheeks. "The most beautiful." She echoed, her voice cracking. "All this time, he was coming to visit her, here in this place. A place only he knew about."

"I wonder if this was their place?" Ben asked. "I like the thought of that. A place that was special to them."

"I like that too," she agreed, looking up at him, adoration in her eyes. "You have been with me throughout this entire journey, and I am so grateful for you. I love you so much, Ben."

He smiled, his eyes crinkling as he wiped the last tear from her cheek. "I love you too, sweetheart."

THAT NIGHT, they melted into each other like they did so well, feeling blissful and satiated.

"I cannot believe I have only one more week left before my summer ends." Ever rested her head on Ben's chest as she ran her fingers through his beard.

"I wish you could stay, sweetheart," he sighed, meeting her eyes. "I cannot imagine spending my days without you."

"I know. I wish I could too." She responded. "But I have a whole life waiting for me in Toronto. A gallery showing my work in a month and friends I have not seen since April."

He nodded in understanding. His throat tightened, a lump of emotion wanting to form. He swallowed down hard as he ran his fingers gently down her bare back. He understood, but the thought of her not being here with him made his heart break. The ache became excruciating as their time ran through the proverbial hourglass of their wonderful summer together.

"You can visit me, and I will come to visit you, Bear. I want to give this long-distance thing a try." she continued meeting his gaze, seeing the emotion in his eyes. "I am not ready to say goodbye to you."

"I am never saying goodbye to you, sweetheart," he declared as he rolled on top of her and captured her face in his hands. "Goodbye is not an option."

His lips crashed into hers, a flood of emotion and desire enfolding them.

CHAPTER 15

Knowing Ever's last weekend at Prairie Sky was upon them, Ben arranged to have a barbeque at the farm with friends, family, and neighbours on Labour Day Weekend – one day ahead of her impending departure. Having kept the secret of Ever's generous gift to himself, they both agreed this was a good time to share it with those that cared for them most.

While Ever busied herself in the kitchen preparing food, Ben prepared the front lawn for the festivities.

Ben slipped into the kitchen and wrapped his arms around her from behind as she was cutting up a carrot for a veggie platter. Swiping a piece of carrot off her cutting board, Ever scolded him. "Hey!"

He wrapped his arm around her waist and kissed up the line of her neck, reaching her ear and giving it a light nip with his teeth.

"Ben, I'm busy here." She giggled, putting the knife down before she cut herself.

He growled and turned her around in his arms, caging

her to the counter, rocking his hard, heavy body against hers seductively. Feeling him hard and ready, she smiled at him through her lashes, giving him a sexy look. Moving aside the cutting board, Ben lifted Ever onto the counter-top, settling himself between her legs. Capturing her lips in a fervent kiss, Ben's hands ran up her legs, sneaking under her dress, finding her already wet with arousal. Running his tongue along her collarbone, he blazed a hot trail with his fingertips under her shirt to cup her breast, running his thumb over the peak.

"Bear, baby," Ever managed to pant out huskily. "People will be here anytime."

He growled and brought his mouth back to hers for a passionate, panty melting kiss, then released their embrace leaving her breathless. "And?" he asked as his fingertips breached her panties to find her insanely aroused. His tongue grazed her upper lip. "I can be quick."

Just then, they heard the front door open, and the unmistakable voice of Bea Baxter echoed through the front entrance. "Hey, you two lovebirds! Where are you?"

Ever's eyes widened as Ben smoothed down her skirt, quickly lifting her off the counter then positioning himself behind her to hide the rather obvious results of their make-out session.

Bea peeked around the corner. "Everyone decent?" she asked with a laugh and a wiggle of her eyebrows. Stepping into the kitchen fully, she put her hands on her hips and gave them an amused smile. "I was actually joking, but I can see by those red faces that I was interrupting something!"

"Come back in an hour." Ben joked, nuzzling his beard

against the side of Ever's face, making her squirm and let out a nervous giggle.

"An hour? Wow, way to go girl!" she raised her hand to Ever for a fist bump. "No can do, you sexy beasts. Hayden just pulled in after me. Everyone else should be here soon."

Ben leaned down to kiss Ever on the cheek and made his way outside to greet his brother and the arriving guests.

Still flushed, Ever grabbed the cutting board and knife and continued her vegetable prep. Bea slid in next to her and put her arm around her for a side hug.

"How are you doing, girl?" Bea asked with a concerned look.

Feeling the emotion, she was trying to tamp down, rise closer to the surface, Ever looked down at Bea, her sadness not able to be hidden. "I've been better. Honestly, I am trying not to think about goodbye."

Bea squeezed her supportively.

"I mean, we're not breaking up or anything and we have mutually agreed to give the long-distance thing a try, but I cannot imagine a day without him now." Ever confessed, letting out a long shaky exhale.

"Do you have to go?" Bea asked.

"I do." Ever replied solemnly. "I have worked so hard to build a life in the city and establish myself in the art community there. I have great relationships with several prominent gallery owners and my apartment, which I love, is there. I feel like if I don't return, I would be giving up a part of me and be giving up on my dream."

"Can't you paint anywhere?"

"Sure." Ever answered. "But if I leave Toronto, I basically start all over again making connections here. I wouldn't even know where to begin."

"I get that," Bea acknowledged. "But have you ever thought that you would give up more by NOT staying? Perhaps your dream has changed or evolved. Perhaps you are not giving up anything at all, just adding more to it. You need to ask yourself: Is what I am giving up worth it, or do I already have everything I need?"

Ever looked down at her friend with surprise and smiled, thinking of the words her mother offered her in her dream. *Did I tell Bea about the words my mother told me in my dream? No, only Ben knows.* She shook her head and put her arm around her friend. "Bea, I love you."

"Love you too! I just want what's best for you."

"Thank you, I know that. I need to return to Toronto and see things through. I owe that to myself."

"I get it girl! But please visit. That country boy of yours is going to be one lonely, sad sack while you're gone."

Ever thought about Ben and how leaving tomorrow would feel? An excruciating pain formed in her chest. The thought of leaving was too much, and she needed to steady her emotions. This week, in the moments she was alone, she cried, feeling lost in her thoughts, and bound to her decisions. She knew what she was doing was best for her but was it going to be best for them? She didn't know. What she did know was that saying goodbye tomorrow would be one of the hardest things she would ever have to do.

* * *

MAKING HER WAY OUTSIDE, Ever halted in her tracks, taking in the scene in front of her. Ben set up a long family style table in the middle of the yard, dressed in a white tablecloth, and little bouquets of Daisies alternating with candles gracing the tabletop. From the posters of the porch, Ben strung fairy lights crisscrossing the yard, that were held up on the other side by temporary tent posts. A temporary wooden dance floor was set up as well. It was like a dream and Ever felt her heart swell at the beauty of it all. Coming down the porch, she was greeted by Hayden, Ms. Lynette, Mr. Estes and his wife and all the friends both old and new she spent time with this summer. Finding Ben off in the corner by the grill, she strolled over to him and put her arms around his neck, reaching up to kiss him softly.

"Did you do all this?" she asked, love and gratitude in her eyes.

"I did. Well, Hayden helped me get the lights up, but yes, I did."

"Oh, Bear, I love it so much. I love you so much too. Thank you."

"Anything for you, sweetheart," he commented, capturing her mouth in a scorching kiss, not caring if they had an audience.

"Get a room!" Hayden bellowed across the yard, causing everyone to turn to them, then whistle and cat call.

Ben laughed and lifted her into his arms for another chaste kiss, then set her down on her feet to continue his grilling.

"Looks good." she offered a glance at the grill. Giving

him a playful slap on the rear, then with a wink, turned and strode off to visit with their guests.

* * *

THE DINNER WAS delicious. grilled steak and chicken skewers, potato salad, pasta salad, veggies and for dessert Ms. Lynette's famous peach cobbler, which she declared was in honor of Hardin Wolton as it was his favorite! The echoes of lively conversation and laughter wafted over the yard as they ate and enjoyed fellowship together. It was simply a perfect evening. A perfect end to an unforgettable summer.

"Can I get everyone's attention?" Ever shouted above the chatter as she stood facing everyone at the head of the table and gestured for Ben to join her where she stood. Everyone quieted and turned to face her, curiosity on their faces. "We have some big news to share regarding Prairie Sky Acres. As of tomorrow, Ben will not only be the Manager of Prairie Sky, but he will officially be the new owner!"

The look of surprise and, in some cases, knowing on their friend's faces morphed into cheers. Their friends stood and swarmed them with handshakes, pats on the back, and hugs.

"Well, I think we need a toast!" Bea exclaimed, raising her glass. Everyone raised their glasses in unison.

"May I?" asked Ms. Lynette.

Ever nodded and raised her glass.

"To Prairie Sky! May the future of this farm be bright, beautiful, full of love and incredible memories!"

"Cheers to Prairie Sky!" everyone shouted as they clinked their glasses in excitement.

"I think it's time to celebrate!" Hayden exclaimed, heading over to the dance floor and table he had set up with speakers. "Ms Lynette, let's see those moves!"

As the sun started to set, the fairy lights were turned on, shimmering over the celebration. Rock and country tunes, along with chatter and laughter filled the quiet spaces as the festivities continued. Ever stole a moment to walk down the long driveway as she watched the beautiful prairie sky spin with bands of pink, purple, yellow, and orange. Wrapping her arms around herself, she thought of all that she had experienced this summer. The mysteries, the discoveries, finding her mother, finding Ben. She couldn't help but think about her father. This place she had once associated with so much disappointment and pain was now a place with so many unforgettable memories. Was her father guiding her? Bringing her back to her roots made her truly think about what she wanted for her life. Making her question her dreams and if she could have it all. *Did he bring me to Ben?* Hearing his footfalls behind her, Ben's familiar strong arms enfolded her. She leaned back and rested her head on his chest, letting out a shaky sigh.

"What are you thinking, sweetheart?" he whispered in her ear as they stared towards the dancing sky.

"I am just thinking how wonderful this summer has been and how grateful I am to have met you."

"You make it sound like you will never see me again," he commented, kissing her head affectionately.

"It feels like a goodbye to me." Her voice cracking with emotion.

Ben turned her around and looked deep into her eyes, cupping her face gently in his large hands. His pools of blue held so much promise, love, and conviction in them.

"No, Ever, sweetheart, it's just a see you later. I promise we will see each other."

Ever nodded, a tear escaping. Ben captured it with his thumb as he leaned down and brushed his lips against hers sweetly. Burying herself in his chest, she breathed in deeply, taking in the familiar scent of him, this man she had grown to love so much. This man she could not imagine living without. Knowing that although they were not yet saying goodbye, their goodbye felt inevitable.

AFTER ALL THE guests had left and the moon was high in the sky, Ben and Ever filled her car with the boxes of keepsakes and belongings she planned to take back with her to Toronto. Closing the trunk, they walked hand in hand together up the porch stairs.

"Can we just sit here for a moment?" Ever asked, feeling melancholy.

"Sure."

They sat down on the top step of the stairs and Ben put his arm around Ever. She shivered, and he removed his jean jacket to wrap it around her shoulders. Grateful, Ever gave him an appreciative smile, feeling the burn of tears well in her eyes. Looking down at her hands, she tried to steady her emotions. Putting his hand out, Ben reached for her, and she intertwined her fingers with his. They fit so perfectly together, like her hand was meant to hold his. Looking out onto the yard of her childhood home, the fairy lights were still on and twinkling along with the stars in the prairie night sky. They sat there together in contemplative silence, so many words wanting to be said but left unspoken. Ben pulled her into his chest, his strong protective arms enrobing her in his warmth and protection. The feel of him, his steady heartbeat under her cheek, making her tears fall and a sob escape her throat. Ben's breath hitched, and she knew he was trying to control his own emotions and be strong for her. Pulling her in tighter, he let her cry. No words of consolation, just his tender touch supporting her. When her tears subsided, he lifted her into his arms, and she melted into him. He carried her into the house and up the stairs to her bedroom for their last night together.

BEN'S HEART ached in his chest as he set Ever down on the bed. He loved her with his whole being, and he wanted to show her what this glorious summer had meant to him. Express to her that there would never and could never be anyone else for him. He loved her with his entire mind, body and soul, and she needed to know. Even if it didn't make a difference in her decision tomorrow, he needed to lay it all out for her.

He slowly removed his clothes, then sliding his jacket

off her shoulders, he reached for the hem of her dress and drew it over her head. Unclasping her bra, she lay back on the bed, her hair cascading around her making his breath catch at the sight of her in the moonlight. *So beautiful.* Laying next to her, she turned to face him. Wishing he knew how to give voice to his feelings right now in this moment, neither spoke, just held each other's gaze for what seemed like an eternity and yet like no time had passed at all. Beholden to this woman he loved so deeply, he reached up and smoothed down her hair, running his fingers through the stray tendrils next to her face. The gesture was so tender, her eyes filled with tears. Capturing her emotion, his lips met hers, a kiss so full of love and devotion, he thought his heart would burst. His kiss promised he was hers forever.

She kissed him back with reverence, not wanting to let him go. His hands roamed over her curves, caressing and touching all the places he had grown to know so well. His lips left hers as he dusted feathery kisses over her skin, wanting to taste her sweetness and sear it into his memory.

She reached for him, and he came over her his powerful body hovering over hers. His eyes met hers, glossy with tears, as she gave him a look of pure and honest love. A look he would never forget. His heart broke right then and there, and tears filled his eyes too. Swallowing their emotions, their lips met softly at first and as if a match was lit, the desire ignited in a tangle of emotion and passion. His tongue parting her lips, he slid his tongue against hers, telling her without words he was going to make love to her.

Wrapping her legs around him, she felt him enter her slowly, stretching her, until her heat fully surrounded him. Deep inside her body. Deep inside her heart. Deep inside her soul. They moved together in a steady rhythm as familiar to them now as breathing. Savouring every pang of pleasure their joining offered. Feeling themselves unravel beautifully together they let the wave of pleasure crash over them, drowning themselves in each other's love. Losing a part of themselves to each other as they crashed to the shore. Their souls bound forever.

* * *

WAKING EARLY before dawn had broken, Ever slipped out of bed quietly. Looking down at Ben, who was turned away snoring softly, she smiled sadly. Last night had been in one word; magical. She closed her eyes, envisioning the way he worshipped her body and how they came together so perfectly, their love making a tangle of raw emotion and exquisite passion. She loved Ben, no question, but she knew in the early hours of the morning as they lay together exhausted by their intense emotions, what she needed to do. The tears that flowed over the last few days, both in his arms and privately, made her heart ache unbearably. She could not do this. The pain of saying goodbye to Ben was more than she could bear, and she needed to go. His love and affection made her mind hazy. If she removed herself from him and returned to her life in the city, she could see clearer. Clarity would help her determine what was best for her and her life. Leaving now, without the long sorrowful goodbye would protect both their hearts. She knew it was for the best.

Quietly dressing and stuffing her clothes from last night into her last remaining bag. She tiptoed out of the room and made her way down the stairs, avoiding the spots on the steps she knew would creak under her weight. Entering the kitchen, she saw a bouquet of daisies sitting on the table from last night's festivities, just like the one Ben brought her on their first date. She smiled a sorrowful smile, a raspy sigh escaping her throat. *I hope he will understand,* she thought, too many questions clouding her judgement. She needed to leave quickly before they overtook her. Looking at the envelope in her hands, she propped it against the vase where he was sure to find it. Making her way to the front door, she quieted for a moment, making sure Ben had not woken. The silence was deafening as hot tears pricked her eyes. With one last look at her childhood home, she left through the front door, not sure when or if she would return.

THE NEXT MORNING Ben woke to the familiar sound of birds chirping and rolled over, finding the bed next to him cold. He sat up and looked around the room, checking the clock. 7 a.m. Ever must be downstairs getting together the last of her things. He had slept so soundly after their love making, the memory of her soft body beneath him making his body and his heart flutter with anticipation of seeing her. He got out of bed, slipped on sleep pants, and padded down the stairs, calling her name. "Ever? Sweetheart? Where are you, baby?" Silence was the only reply.

His brow furrowed as he descended the stairs and into the kitchen. She was not there. His eyes caught sight of the daisies on the table and an envelope propped against the vase. As he approached the note, he noticed her endearment for him. "Bear" written on the front. Picking up the note, his stomach fell, and he rubbed his hand over his beard anxiously.

Bear,

This summer has meant more to me than I can even tell you. When I came back to Prairie Sky, I was scared, scared of what I would feel and scared of what I would find. What I found were truths about my family and, most importantly, what I found was you. I love you, Bear. With every part of me. More than I ever thought I could love another person. You have filled my heart with memories and washed away any negativity Prairie Sky held for me in the past. For you, I am truly grateful. I know this is not the way you may have chosen for our goodbye to go, but I know that if I were to look you in the eyes one last time, I could never leave. And I need to leave. I need to see my dream through. I need to return to the life I had worked so hard to build before this glorious summer. I hope that without distraction I can decide what I want my life to look like going forward. As you have said to me several times, this is not good-bye, just a "see you later". Although this letter may seem like a goodbye, after you read my words, I pray it is just a "see you later."

All my love, Ever

Ben shook his head in disbelief as he ran his hand

through his hair in frustration. *She is gone. She is really gone.* He couldn't feel the warmth of her in his arms again or kiss her sweet, soft lips one last time. An excruciating ache bore into his chest. An emptiness so painful he couldn't breathe. Rereading the letter his eyes filled with tears, an agonizing sob escaping. *Last night I had given her everything I had to give, and she still left without saying good-bye?* His pain quickly turned to anger as he slammed his fist down on the kitchen counter, then sank to the floor. His legs folded and his head in his hands. There on that kitchen floor of his farmhouse she gifted him, he wept.

Ever turned down her street, her apartment building coming into view. Getting out of her car, she looked up at the grey sky, overcast and dreary. A reflection of how she felt right now. The drive back to Toronto, long and lonely, making her thoughts drift to Ben. It had been three days on the road, and she had not received a call or text from him. *Have I made a mistake? Was I just trying to protect my heart and, as a result, disregarded his?* Doubting herself, she looked up to the window of her apartment. *Home.*

She looked back and forth on either side, the noise of the open patios of restaurants carrying the sound of voices and laughter and the faint sound of traffic. A vast contrast from the peace and quiet of Prairie Sky. Reaching into her car, she retrieved two duffle bags, turning around to lock her doors with her key fob. As she was about to enter her building, a familiar voice sounded behind her.

"You're here!"

Looking to the side, she saw the familiar face of Whitney Faris. Her shoulder-length blonde hair bobbing as she ran down the street to meet Ever. She was dressed stylishly as always, in a pair of form fitted dark wash jeans, white t-shirt and a purple fitted blazer. Undoubtedly coming from work. Her brown eyes beamed at her friend.

"Hey Whitney!" Ever acknowledged her with a big hug. "I wasn't expecting you here! How are you doing?"

"Awesome! So glad you're back! Ever, you look amazing!" she appraised as she held her out to look at her. "You look so tanned and gorgeous! Farm life was good to you?"

Ever laughed, shrugged, and gave her a tired grin.

"Tired though, eh? Long drive?"

"Yes, very long drive." she sighed, slumping her shoulders forward.

"Okay, let's get your stuff inside! I can help, then maybe we can order some food?"

"That sounds fantastic.", Ever replied, grateful for her friend's forethought.

Handing her bags to Whitney, she retrieved a large box from her trunk, and they made their way up the stairs. Unlocking the door, she entered her unassuming loft apartment. Her queen size bed was off in the back corner, opposite the corner kitchen and in the makeshift living room area a small couch, coffee table, bookshelves filled with art books and a desk. The large window overlooked the street, bringing in lots of natural light. Her easel and a canvas set up by the window along with a rolling work cart holding brushes, palettes, and a menagerie of paints.

Her place was small, but cozy, and looked the same as when she left it. *Was it always this small?*

It took several trips to get all the boxes up the stairs, but the friends finally flopped down on the couch exhausted, feeling accomplished. Taking out her phone, Whitney ordered their dinner from their favorite bistro and leaned over the coffee table, peeking into the box they had set down there.

"So, what is all this stuff?" Whitney inquired.

"Keepsakes, mostly my dad's stuff, things I just could not give away."

Whitney nodded and slumped back onto the couch. "I know we didn't talk much while you were away other than work stuff." She continued gesturing to Ever's easel. "But did you get some closure regarding your dad?"

"Mostly," she answered. "I had questions about my mother answered and a better understanding of why my dad told me to leave Prairie Sky, but there were so many mysteries, it was kind of hard to unpack everything."

Whitney turned to her and gave her a sympathetic smile. "Families can be complicated sometimes, and sometimes people hold secrets for a reason, whether it is understandable to others or just to them. Perhaps it makes no sense to you now, but maybe someday it will all become clear." She offered.

"True." Ever agreed.

They sat there together for a few minutes in quiet contemplation. The buzzer of her apartment sounded, startling them both, and Whitney sprang to her feet. Buzzing the delivery guy in, she paid for their food and brought it to the kitchen counter. Plating their meals, she returned to Ever on the couch and handed her a plate.

"Now tell me about that hot farmer you fell for!" Whitney grinned, taking a bite of her sandwich.

Ever smiled, set down her plate on the coffee table and met Whitney's gaze. "You saw how handsome he is, but he is so much more than that. Just so selfless, supportive, and kind. He looks so large and intimidating, but he is so soft and gentle. He made me feel so safe and loved I..." Ever trailed off as she swiped a tear sliding down her cheek.

Whitney put down her plate and reached out to her friend, bringing her in for a hug. "Oh Ever, don't cry."

"I messed it up. I think I made a mistake." Ever cried into Whitney's shoulder.

"Did you break up?" Whitney asked, meeting Ever's eyes.

"No, but..." she replied, lowering her eyes. "The day I left to come home; I just could not do it. It was far too painful. I left him a note and a promise that I would try to figure out what I wanted.

"So, you never actually said goodbye to one another?" Whitney asked, her eyes wide.

"I knew that if I had to say a last goodbye that I would never leave him."

"Hmmm… and you both decided to try a long-distance relationship?" she questioned.

"Yes, although I haven't heard from him yet," she replied. "Not sure how he took my note. I haven't had any calls or texts."

"You don't want my opinion on this, do you?" Whitney asked, folding her arms over her chest.

One thing Ever loved about her friend was her blunt honesty. She always gave good advice, even if it hurt to hear. "Shoot." Ever replied, bracing herself against the back of the couch.

"I think he needs time to understand why you would leave without saying goodbye to him. He is likely heartbroken." Whitney offered. "Even if you spelled it out for him in that note, your actions carry more weight than your words."

Ever put her head back on the couch cushion and sighed. "So, you think I screwed things up?"

Whitney shook her head. "Not necessarily, but you have probably wounded him. The question is, how deep?"

Ever had never thought of it that way. She thought by leaving the way she did, she was sparing them both more pain. *How am I going to proceed now?*

BEN SAT in the emergency room waiting room, his hand swollen and bruised. Feeling sad, lost, and sheepish, he knew he was the reason he was there now. When he read Ever's note, his sadness, frustration and disappointment came out in anger and now he had a damaged hand to show for it. *Idiot*, he thought. Stubbornly he bandaged it up and tried to go about his days, but it hurt too much, both his hand and his heart.

"Ben?" the front desk nurse asked.

"Yes." he rose out of his chair and strode to the Emergency Room desk.

"Come with me," said the nurse.

She led him through the back to triage and into a little area in the corner enclosed by a curtain and gestured for him to have a seat on the hospital bed. He sat there, his head down, cradling his hand as he continued to wait. Suddenly the curtain pulled back, startling him and he was greeted by the familiar face of Bea Baxter.

"Hey BB." he acknowledged with swollen, red-rimmed eyes.

"Ben, you look like shit, my friend!" she exclaimed, hands on her hips as she met his vacant stare.

"I feel like shit too," he agreed. "Pretty sure I broke my hand."

Bea approached him and examined his hand, eyebrows raised she looked at him in question. "What the hell did you do?"

"The kitchen countertop…" he hesitated. "I slammed my hand down on the countertop."

Bea winced and looked up at Ben, her eyes softening with kindness. "What got you so upset, Benny? You're a chill guy. It's not like you to act out like that."

Ben met her gaze, his face turning red and his eyes shining with tears.

"Oh." Bea whispered knowingly and put her hand on his shoulder in a sympathetic gesture. "Let's get you over to X-ray and see what the damage is."

* * *

BEN SAT on the old leather couch, a sports channel on mute and a beer in his only good hand. He heard a car come up the driveway, a car door slam followed by footsteps on the porch. Not wanting to get up to go see who was there, he sank further into the couch. Hearing a sharp knock on the door, a pause and the door latch open, he growled. He must have forgotten to lock the door.

"Hey Bro!" a familiar voice sounded from behind him. Hayden came around the couch and stood in front of his brother. "Dude, you look like shit."

"Yeah, that seems to be the consensus." He growled, giving his brother an annoyed glare.

"Bea called me saying she's worried about you. Saying you messed up your hand?" he asked, pointing to the bandage covering his hand.

"Yeah, hairline fracture." Ben confirmed, holding up his splintered hand.

"Damn." Hayden commented as he ran his hand through his hair and took a seat next to him on the couch before continuing, "Does this have anything to do with Ever leaving?"

Ben gave his brother a sideways glance and gestured to the coffee table where her note to him sat.

Picking up the letter, Hayden began to read it, his eyebrows raising. "Wow, Ben, I'm so sorry," he said, looking up and giving his brother a pitiful look. "Do you think she is going to come back?"

"I have no idea."

"Did you try to contact her?" he questioned.

"No," he growled and took a swig of his beer letting the liquid numb his emptiness.

"Well, that's your first problem, then!" Hayden exclaimed. "You need to get clarification."

"What's not clear?" Ben asked, rising from the couch

and pacing the floor in front of it. "She said I am a distraction; I distract her from her dream and the life she wants!" He stopped and ran his hand through his beard in frustration.

"That's not how I see it, Ben." Hayden offered.

"How do you goddamn see it, then? Because all I see is that I have lost her completely!" Ben shot back, complete anguish on his face.

"Settle down Bro." Hayden encouraged, patting the couch where Ben had been sitting. Ben sank to the couch, utter defeat washing over him. Leaning forward, he ran his uninjured hand through his hair.

"I want to marry her, Hayden. Get hitched, have kids, the white picket fence, the whole thing," he confessed, looking at his brother with sorrowful eyes, glossy with tears.

Hayden reached out, putting his hand on Ben's shoulder in reassurance, and they sat there in silence for a few minutes. Breaking the silence, Hayden offered his advice. "I would give her a few weeks, but honestly, bro, I would go to her."

"Go to Toronto?" Ben asked, his eyebrows shooting up in question.

"Yes." Hayden smiled. "Have you ever heard of a grand gesture?"

* * *

THE NEXT THREE weeks dragged out with no word from Ben. Ever tried to go about her days, but he consumed her thoughts. *Was he mad? Was he hurt?* Her note was not a breakup, just a slow down. Just a moment to breathe and figure out what she really wanted. She didn't know how to proceed, and the radio silence from him was deafening.

To keep herself busy, she started the task of emptying the boxes she had brought with her. Her father's keepsakes, pictures, and some of her childhood belongings. She opened the box with her father's favorite books and ran her hands over their titles, thinking of him. *Oh, how he loved these.* Picking up the *Catcher in the Rye*, she held it in her hands and smoothed over its cover. Remembering her father's journal and his entry mentioning the book and the first time he spoke to her mother. She smiled as she opened the book, the PRIMROSE HIGH SCHOOL stamp in the front cover. She noticed a page bent over and turned to it. Underlined was a quote:

"I think that one of these days," he said, "you're going to have to find out where you want to go. And then you've got to start going there. But immediately. You can't afford to lose a minute. Not you."

Ever read the words out loud, letting them soak in and looked down at the book again. A little corner of white paper peeked out of another part of the book. *What's this?* She thought, pulling it out and opening it. It read:

Ever,

If you are reading this, I am gone. You have probably found my journal and understand how important this book is to me.

Before this dusty old cowboy gets too sappy,

I want you to know I am sorry. The day you left Prairie Sky, I said things, hurtful things, things that I am certain broke your heart. I have no excuse for the angry words I said, other than to say my words were those of a protective father wanting to keep his daughter close. Having you here on the farm made me feel closer to your mother. Did I ever tell you that you look like her? So beautiful. I miss her, Ever. Every single day. She left us too soon. The day you left to pursue your dreams, the day you left and vowed to never return, it felt like she died all over again. I felt guilty holding you back, but I was selfish. I was selfish about so many things. I selfishly changed your name (which you have probably figured out already). Your mother named you after her in some ways. Violet and Daisy, a perfect bouquet, she would say. I would call you my flowers. When she died, I shut down. Hearing your birth name made the loss of your mother worse. It made the cut deeper. It is something I am not proud of, so I kept it from you. Again, I am sorry. I am sorry for so many things.

You have probably already figured out that your mother was an artist, too. I would love to watch her draw when I could. When the busyness of farm life allowed me to. Oh, how she loved to draw. She would be so proud of you and your successes. I am proud of you Ever. I know I never told you, and for that I am sorry. Ms. Lynette showed me how to use Google on the computer and I searched for your name. Yes, this old dog can be taught new tricks! I even have one of your pieces hanging in my office. Not going to tell you what I paid, but I can tell you I sold 3 sheep at auction to afford that painting. Art is expensive. Worth every penny, though. Looking at that painting made me think of your mom and of you. It made me feel closer to you both and if I could picture heaven, it looks like you're painting. Knowing that I will someday sit on that bench with my sweet flower again gives me peace.

I wanted to see you many times. I bought tickets to fly to Toronto but cancelled them each time. Before I knew it, before I mustered enough courage, too much time had passed. You had grown, your life was so different from life on the farm. I was scared. Felt guilty. I was not sure if you wanted to see me. My fears kept me here at Prairie Sky, watching you from afar, wishing our relationship was different. Wanting to hug you, my sweet daughter, and promise to be the father you needed me to be. Again, I am so very sorry. I love you, my girl. Despite my harsh words and actions, you are always in my heart and part of my soul. I am proud of the woman you have become. So strong and independent. No matter how old you get, you will always be my sunshine and all the stars at night, just like I would tell you as a little girl.

And my sweet Ever, if you are lucky enough to find true love, go to it, cherish it, hold on to it with all that you have. Because true love is not just a feeling, it's a sacrifice.

Love You always.

Daddy

Shaking, Ever cupped her mouth, letting a sob escape, tears trailing down her face. Her father's last words to her, all the things that were unsaid between them. Everything she needed so desperately to hear. Clarity washed over her as she now knew exactly where she belonged and who she belonged with. *Would Ben want me back, or had I broken him too much?*

* * *

WALKING INTO THE EAZY, Ben immediately spotted Hayden and Bea sitting in a far corner of the café waiting for him.

"Hey guys," he acknowledged, taking a seat across from them.

"Hey Big Ben! Thanks for showering for us and cleaning yourself up a bit," Bea teased, giving him a compassionate smile. "You're looking a lot better than the last time I saw you."

"Yeah, you definitely look a lot better, bro." Hayden agreed. "Have you been thinking about my suggestion?"

"I have." Ben replied with a nod. "Just not sure exactly what I should do."

Bea beamed with excitement. "Hayden filled me in, and I think a grand gesture is exactly the right course of action. If you have not figured it out yet, Ever is a hope-less romantic, but she is practical too. She loves you. There is no question there. I know she wants to be with you at Prairie Sky, but she is scared to give up the life she has established in the city." Bea explained.

Ben nodded in agreement.

"You need to show her it is a sacrifice worth making. You need to show her you are willing to give up your dreams for her. If she sees you are willing to sacrifice what is important to you for her, putting her first above all else, I know she is going to want to do the same for you." Bea continued knowingly.

"So, what exactly do you think I should do?" Ben asked.

"You go to her, and you tell her you are moving to be close to her." Hayden suggested. "I know that is not what you want, but wouldn't you do anything and give up all you have to be with her?"

"Everything." Ben confirmed in agreement. "Even Prairie Sky, if that is what she wants."

Both Bea and Hayden smiled as they glanced at each other.

"Then we know exactly what you should do." Bea answered, sliding a piece of paper across the table.

Ben picked up the paper and his eyes widened as he flashed them a confirming smile.

Reaching for Ben's hand, Bea gave it a confident squeeze and met his gaze. "Go get your girl."

CHAPTER 17

*E*ver entered the trendy downtown gallery and took in the sign at the front door. "Prairie Musings - the works of Ever Wolton" on a large sign. Smiling proudly, she slipped her jacket off her shoulders, revealing her daisy dress, the same dress she wore on her first date with Ben. When deciding what to wear for this event, the beautiful dress was the only choice that made sense. Smoothing down the skirt, she spotted Whitney, who gave her a wave of acknowledgement and strode over to greet her. Whitney, dressed in a green cocktail dress, makeup, and hair on point, looked every bit the professional. She hugged Ever and held her arms out to look at her.

"Ever you are gorgeous tonight. That dress is amazing!"

"Thank you" Ever smiled, smoothing her hands over the embroidered daisies along the neckline. Her mind drifted to Ben and his face the first time he saw her in this dress. *Oh, how I miss that smile and those beautiful blue eyes.*

"Are you ready, my friend?" Whitney asked, turning towards the sign.

Nervously, Ever let out a deep breath. "I think so. Never thought I would be back here again."

"Tonight will be fantastic!" Whitney reassured, giving her another squeeze. "We are expecting a full house tonight as there is so much buzz about your new work. Seriously, these may be your best paintings yet. I know they will all sell."

Giving her friend a look of gratitude, Ever followed Whitney into the gallery, making her way towards the Gallery Director who shook her hand as she gushed about her paintings.

As the doors opened, the gallery filled. Friends and acquaintances, faces old and new mingled happily, wine flowing, appetizers making the rounds and Ever, working the room sharing her thoughts and inspirations for each piece on display. The high of compliments surrounding her made her feel back in her element. Despite this, her thoughts continued to drift to Ben, wishing he was here with her. Roaming through the gallery, she stopped at her favorite painting in her collection. "The Protector". The silhouette of Ben, golden and beautiful, leaning on the porch railing, coffee in hand, taking in all that is now his. She remembered the day she painted this, how he allowed her to capture this moment. The protector of Prairie Sky, the protector of her heart. Her eyes welled up as she remembered the warmth of his strong arms around her. That feeling of completeness in his embrace. She took a deep breath and let it out slowly, trying to steady her emotions.

Just then, she felt a hand on her shoulder, which startled her from her reflections. Turning around to see Whitney beaming with excitement. "Sorry to startle you, but your first piece just sold!" she shared brightly.

"Which one?" Ever asked, looking around the room.

Whitney gestured to "The Protector" and Ever's heart sank, unexpected disappointment coming over her in a wave. "Who purchased it?" she asked, looking around the room again.

Just as she asked her question, she saw him. Standing across the room, towering over the guests, eyes transfixed on hers. As devastatingly handsome as she remembered him. Dressed in a blue button-down shirt, black jeans, and a brown leather jacket with matching cowboy boots. He looked like a dream. He smiled the gorgeous smile she loved so much, his bright blue eyes shining. Drawing her in like a beacon, like a ship in a storm. He strode to her, the crowd parting like something in a movie.

Whitney leaned over to her and whispered. "Follow your heart," then stepped aside.

Ever let out a long breath she didn't realize she was holding as Ben reached her and stopped a mere foot apart away. Her gaze locked on his. He looked down on her tenderly, making her knees weak and her heart flutter wildly.

"Hello." Ben said, his hands in his pockets, a look of uncertainty on his face. "I hope it's okay that I'm here?" he continued. "I missed you and don't want to spend another day without you. I am here indefinitely if you will have me."

Ever just stared at him, her eyes locked in on him, no

words being said between them. Awkward silence clouded over them as they just stood so close, but not reaching out to one another.

"I will sell the farm, move here, whatever you want or need. I will give up everything just to be with you."

Ever's lips slowly curved up in a smile. Stepping closer, her body flush with his, Ever put her arms around his neck, searching his eyes. "You had me at Hello, Bear."

Ben threw back his head, his deep bountiful laugh echoing through the now quiet gallery. His arms enveloped her as he lifted her and swung her around, relief washing over them both. Setting her down. he took her face into his hands and lowered his lips to hers in a reunion embrace full of passion and love.

Clapping and catcalls broke their seemingly private moment. Ever looked around at everyone's smiling faces and immediately spotted Hayden and Bea walking up, whistling and clapping. Her eyes widened in joy and surprise as she hugged them both. "I can't believe you are both here!"

"We wouldn't miss this for the world!" Bea exclaimed excitedly.

"Absolutely." Hayden agreed.

Bringing her attention back to Ben, she reached up and kissed him again as she ran her fingers through his beard affectionately. "Did you really buy my painting?"

"I did," Ben replied, taking her hands in his. "I know it was your favorite and perhaps we can hang it in *our* home."

Touching his face, she caressed his cheek and looked deeply into his eyes. "You don't have to move here, Bear. I have already decided to come to you. Prairie Sky is my home, it always has been, and I want to be with you. It's where we both belong together, and I am sorry it took me a while to realize that."

Ben smiled as he mirrored her affectionate caress. Ever closed her eyes and leaned into his loving touch. His hand leaving her face, she opened her eyes to see Ben down on one knee in front of her. Looking up with love and expectation in his hopeful blue eyes. "Ever Wolton, I want to drink coffee with you every morning and make love to you every night. I want to build a life, a family and grow old with you. Sitting on our front porch, taking in every prairie sunset. I love you and I want to make every dream you have come true. Will you marry me?" Ben asked, reaching into his pocket and pulling out a small velvet box.

Releasing her hand, he opened the box, presenting it to her. Looking down, Ever's eyes met the most beautiful gold band with diamonds shaped like a daisy. Ever put her hand to her mouth, blinking back her tears. Meeting his expectant gaze, seeing her future within its depths, she answered. "Yes, Bear, I will marry you!" she exclaimed, a shaky laugh escaping. "I want to spend forever with you!"

Cheers erupted throughout the gallery as he slipped the unique ring on her finger. She looked down, taking in his choice and knowing it was simply perfect. As unique as their love story.

Ben held Ever in his arms, both naked, their bodies tangled around each other, basking in the glow of their reunion. Her head melted into his chest; she reached up to run her fingers through his beard, making him close his eyes in satisfaction.

"Feel good?" she asked huskily.

"So good," he growled, pulling her up to his lips for a passionate embrace.

She moved on top of him, straddling his hips. Their mouths still connected, their tongues dancing together. Ever released their kiss and Ben took in a deep breath, looking up at his beautiful fiancée.

"I have missed you so much." He confessed. "I am sorry it took me so long to come to you."

Ever leaned over and kissed him again softly. "Bear, you came at the perfect time. I cannot wait to marry you."

"Whenever you are ready, sweetheart," he replied, flipping her over and underneath him. "You just tell me the date."

She put her index finger to her chin, tapping it as if in thought. "How about in three weeks? A fall wedding?"

"Will that give you enough time to plan?" he asked, hovering over her, their eyes transfixed.

"Bear, all I need is you and I and a few friends to witness."

Ben brushed his lips against hers and met her gaze with a mischievous grin. "Sounds good to me. The sooner we get married, the sooner we can have all those cute babies you want."

"How about we start now?" she asked, raising her eyebrow offering him a wicked smile.

His lips curved up slowly, and a low growl escaped his throat. "Yes, ma'am!"

* * *

Taking in her reflection, Ever ran her hands down her wedding dress, her mother's wedding dress. Once the news of their engagement and her permanent return to Prairie Sky hit the Primrose gossip mill, Ms. Lynette contacted her immediately regarding her mother's dress. At the request of her mother, Ms. Lynette kept the dress, in safe keeping to one day give back to Ever. Ever was thrilled, and the dress was perfect! A sweetheart neckline dress with a simple A-line skirt, with long lace sleeves and floral appliques that cascaded down the skirt. It was exactly what she would have picked. Her mahogany hair swept up with tendrils of her wavy hair framing her face and fall flowers interwoven, completed her wedding day look. She was ready.

"You look incredible," Bea chimed behind her. "Your parents would have been so proud." She continued with her hand on Ever's shoulder.

Ever met her friend's eyes in the mirror. She knew both her parents were there in spirit with her. They had brought her back here, helped guide her through her self-discovery and now were smiling down on her as she was about to marry the love of her life.

Making their way out of her room and down the stairs, Ms. Lynette met them in the front entrance handing her a beautiful bouquet of fall foliage tied with a violet ribbon. An homage to her mother.

"You look gorgeous, darlin'." She cooed, giving her a kiss on the cheek. "Everyone is here, so whenever you are ready."

Ever nodded as Ms. Lynette slipped out to join the rest of the guests on the lawn. The processional music began and Ever smiled. "Amazed" by Lonestar, their song. The song they danced to when they first kissed. The night she knew. The night her life was forever changed.

Giving her a wink, Bea smoothed down her violet dress and walked down the aisle, joining Ben and Hayden at the end.

Ever stepped out onto the porch, the scene in front of her making her breath catch. The aisle was lined with candles and jars full of fall flowers. The walkway was flagged on both sides with hay bales, covered in burlap for seating. At the end of the aisle was a beautiful carved trellis Hayden built as a wedding gift to them. Fall foliage cascaded from the top and flowed down the sides. The late afternoon prairie sky hung before her, shimmering in bands of pink, orange, and gold. She had never seen anything more beautiful. It was everything she dreamed of and more.

Making her way down the stairs, everyone rose as she started down the aisle. Halfway down, Ben stepped forward dressed handsomely in a tailored navy suit, a crisp white shirt underneath, no tie. An easy style that suited him. Her eyes locked with his beautiful blue eyes that shone with tears. Reaching him, he took her in. "You are stunning." He whispered, putting out his hand, then leading her to the end of the aisle.

Turning to each other, he took both her hands in his.

Looking down, she remembered the first time she noticed her small hand in his large one. The day they met five months ago. An unexpected stranger and now someone she could not live without. A full circle.

Mr. Estes, also a local marriage commissioner, looked at them both, giving them an approving smile.

"Welcome friends and family here to this beautiful place, where we have the privilege and honor of witnessing the marriage of Ben Hastings to Ever Wolton. Two incredible people who were brought together by grief and circumstance and found a love bigger than this prairie sky before us."

Ben looked at Ever and smiled as they looked at the stunning view before them.

"And now for your vows." Mr. Estes said, putting his hand on both of their shoulders, then taking a step back. "Ben?"

Ben pulled out a paper from the inside pocket of his jacket, unfolding it carefully. His eyes rose to hers, the endearing creases deepening as he smiled at her; so much love and warmth within them.

"Ever, I'm not sure what I did in this lifetime to deserve the love of a woman like you. A woman so beautiful, unique, talented, creative, loving, compassionate and funny, this simple man is humbled that you have chosen to be with me." Ben's deep voice cracked as a tear rolled down his cheek.

Ever reached up to catch it with her thumb and gave him a smile to continue.

"You have painted my life with color, and I look forward to the picture we are going to create together. I will love and cherish you always, sweetheart, from this day until we are old and grey."

Ever's eyes welled up with tears as she dabbed them with her hands and laughed. "That was perfect, Bear."

Ben beamed as he stuffed his paper back into his jacket pocket.

Ever cleared her throat and looked up at the love of her life, seeing forever in his eyes as she deadpanned. "You had me at hello."

Their guests erupted in a mingle of laughter and tears.

Ben laughed as Ever held up her hand to continue, quieting their guests.

"From that first hello on the back deck, I knew that my life would never be the same. I am not sure I have words to fully describe what you mean to me and how much I love you. You are my favorite part of every day, and you are the dream I always hoped to have. I love you today and know I will love you more tomorrow. Said simply, "You complete me."

Ben beamed at her, his eyes shining with love and devotion for her.

"Rings?" Mr. Estes asked.

Hayden handed two bands to him, and he handed one to Ben first.

"I, Ben Hastings, take you, Ever Wolton, to be my wife. I will stand by you through all of life's triumphs and challenges and I vow to be faithful to you all the days of my life." Slipping the band on Ever's finger, he smiled with joy radiating.

"I, Ever Wolton, take you, Ben Hastings, to be my husband. I will stand by you through all of life's triumphs and challenges and I vow to be faithful and loving to you all the days of my life," She vowed, sliding the gold band onto Ben's finger.

"By the power vested in me by the Province of Manitoba, I am excited to pronounce you officially married! Ben, you may kiss your wife!"

Ever jumped into his arms and Ben crashed his lips to hers as he swung his beautiful wife around. Their family and friends exploded in cheers for the happy couple.

Setting Ever down on her feet, he intertwined his hand with hers. "Are you ready for forever, Mrs. Hastings?"

"Yes" Ever nodded and looked toward the heavens above, knowing that their angels were watching over them as the magnificent prairie sky, in all its glorious colors, danced in celebration.

5 Years later

EVER SET down her paintbrush and palette. Giving her canvas a sideways look, she took in the vibrant colors of her latest commissioned piece. After returning to Prairie Sky Acres 5 years ago, and marrying the love of her life, she opened a gallery in St. Augustine where local artisans could display their various works. This gallery became a passion project and the connections she made locally, very soon kept her busy with commission paintings.

It's coming together nicely; she thought as she rubbed her growing baby belly and felt it press against her hands.

"Hello Baby Boy," she whispered, smoothing over where her unborn son just made his presence known.

Eight months pregnant, she felt huge, and her feet ached in the prairie summer heat. It was a hot one today, and she had been standing in front of her easel for the past hour. Lowering herself carefully onto her mother's bench, she let out a deep breath and wiped the sweat beading on her forehead with the back of her hand. Reaching for her Sun Tea she took a long sip, letting the refreshing drink cool her. "That's better." She sighed as she held the cold glass to her head.

Pregnancy had not always been easy for Ever, this being her third in five years. Shortly after their wedding, Ever discovered she was pregnant. Shortly after that finding out they were expecting twins. A difficult pregnancy ensued with bed rest, but just seven months after their wedding, their beautiful pink bundles arrived, healthy and happy. Eighteen months ago, they found out they were expecting again, and they were thrilled. However, after ten weeks, she miscarried, devastating them both. A few months later, they decided to try one more time to grow their family and before long they were expecting. Their rainbow pregnancy had proceeded without complications and once they found out they were expecting a boy, Ben could not contain his excitement. Their family felt complete.

Familiar giggles echoed through the yard, drawing closer. Two rosy-cheeked little girls, her four-year-old identical twins, Violet and Poppy, rounded the side of the house both proudly carrying kittens from the barn.

"Hello, you two! You look like you've had fun helping Daddy with the chores." she remarked, taking in their dusty clothes and sweet faces covered in sweat and dirt. They both nodded, their reddish-brown ponytails bobbing. "What have you got here?" she asked, taking in the cute balls of fur in their arms.

"Mama, we have kittens!" Poppy offered, her blue eyes dancing with delight as she held out an orange kitten to Ever.

"Daddy says we can keep them! Aren't they cute?" Violet asked as she pet her purring little tabby.

"Oh, he did, did he?"

"I did", a deep voice sounded as Ben came around the corner. His face beamed as he looked to their little girls and then flashed Ever his smoldering smile, those creases by his eyes still making her heart flip. T-shirt stuffed in his back pocket and work pants sitting low on his hips, making her breath catch at the sight of her very sexy husband.

Giving Ben a mischievous grin, she unabashedly surveyed his muscular tanned chest, stomach, and the tantalizing V at his hips making her mouth water. *How is it he gets hotter and hotter?* Five years of marriage and she still thought he was the most gorgeous man she had ever seen. He still starred in all her fantasies. Amorous thoughts like that got her into this predicament, looking down at her huge baby belly. *Seriously, these pregnancy hormones are crazy*, she thought, shaking her head.

Swooping their girls into his arms, he gave them both a big hug and tickled their faces with his beard making them giggle and wriggle in his arms. Ever loved seeing him with Poppy and Violet. His love and affection for his "flowers" as he affectionately called them, always made a lump form in her throat. She would always think of her late father.

She still missed her dad and over the years would go for a ride so she could talk to him. She would visit her mother's resting place and the summer after they discovered her mothers grave, they laid her father to rest there too, spreading his ashes in their favorite place.

Setting the girls down, they skipped down the stairs to the lawn where they settled down in the grass to play with their kittens.

Transfixing his steely blue gaze on Ever, he gave her a sympathetic look and frowned as he climbed the porch stairs. "You look tired, Sweetheart."

"Just hot, Bear." she replied, dabbing her forehead.

He smiled and leaned down to softly brush his lips to hers. She parted her lips letting him deepen his kiss and run his tongue alongside hers. She sighed and melted into his embrace. He always had a way of making her forget all her troubles. His musky male scent made her hormones go crazy again, she broke their kiss and raked her eyes over him, her eyes hooded and needy. Meeting his gaze, she seductively bit her bottom lip the way she knew drove him crazy.

"Don't give me that look, sweetheart." Ben laughed, shaking his head as he slipped in next to her on the bench.

"What look?" she questioned giving him a flirtatious grin while batting her eyelashes.

"Oh, you know what I'm talking about Ever, that sexy let's go upstairs look." he replied with a smirk and a raised eyebrow. "That look that says I want to do dirty, nasty things to you farm boy."

"Yeah, pretty sure that look got us Junior, here." she laughed pointing to her protruding belly, then winced and rubbed over where their son had just kicked her.

"Not that I mind" he offered, giving her a wink and a waggle of his eyebrows. "How is our son doing today?" he asked placing his large hand lovingly over her huge bump.

"Almost cooked. Three weeks to go. He's been very active today."

Ben slipped off the bench and going to his knees put both of his large hands on her burgeoning belly. Suddenly their little one kicked, and Ben smiled up at her beaming. "That never gets old." he whispered, rubbing his hand over her bump as he smiled up at Ever, a look of pure reverence on his face.

"Tell that to my body." she replied, leaning back on the bench. "This barefoot and pregnant thing is not easy."

"Oh sweetheart." He sympathized, then leaned down and kissed her bump with such tenderness, tears formed in her eyes. "Have I told you how beautiful you are today?" he asked, meeting her gaze.

"Yes."

"Have I told you I love you?"

"Every day, Bear, every single day." She replied, eyes shining with happiness.

"Then let me tell you one more thing." He took her face tenderly in his hands and brushing his lips gently to hers. "Thank you. Thank you for choosing us and this beautiful life."

Tears escaped Ever's eyes, and he caught a tear with his thumb as he caressed her cheek. She leaned into his caress and closed her eyes. Every dream she ever imagined had come true, just as he had promised and never once had she regretted her choice.

Ben settled back down next to her on the bench wrapping his strong arms around her, protectively pulling her closer. Enveloped in his loving embrace her head melted into his chest as they looked out over their beautiful family they had created. Reflecting on this incredible life they built together and all the blessings their life had given them. Forever dreaming of the future with the afternoon sun high in the endless prairie sky.

* * *

Thank you for reading Prairie Sky.
Want more steamy romance set in the idyllic town of
Primrose?
Read Prairie Nights now!

The Spring of Love Series
By Virginia Taylor
Forever Delighted

Forever Amused

Forever Heartfelt

A New Page

by Aimee MacRae

It Happened in Paris

By Michelle Beesley

Middle Women

By Jack Garrety

Mim and Wiggy's Grand Adventure

By Jay McKenzie

A Dying Second Sun

by Peter A. Dowse

Winner Winner Chicken Dinner

by Sarah Jackson

Resurrection

M H Austin

For more information visit:

www.serenadepublishing.com

ABOUT THE AUTHOR

Tanya Renee is a proud Canadian Prairie girl, who grew up on a family farm in Southeastern Manitoba Canada. Always an avid reader, she became intrigued with the romance genre at an early age when she first read Romeo and Juliet. Soon after she started to craft her own stories and poetry and by the time she was in high school, she had declared someday she would become a writer.

Married to the love of her life, she resides in Steinbach, Manitoba, Canada with two teenagers and a menagerie of pets. A kitchen consultant by day and romance writer by night, when she is not cooking up a storm in my kitchen, she can be found tinkering in her garden, drinking copious amounts of coffee with a book in hand, listening to 80's music/audiobooks or at her laptop creating stories that are emotionally satisfying. She writes what she wants to read, epic stories that bring you on a journey and make you believe in love.

www.tanyareneeromance.com

ACKNOWLEDGMENTS

I would like to acknowledge the wonderful teachers at Landmark Collegiate, who encouraged me to read voraciously and share my creativity with the world. Specifically, my 7th grade teacher, Mrs. Ruth Moon, who told me I had a voice, and I should use it. It may have taken me a long time to finally share it with the world, but your kind words have never left me.

To the wonderful community of Landmark, Manitoba that inspired my fictional town of Primrose. A place I am so proud to come from.

To my family farm, Lynette Acres. You may no longer be in the family, but you are forever in my heart.

To my Parents, who always encouraged me to be myself and the rest would follow. I appreciate and love you so much. Specifically, to my dad, the OG dusty cowboy in this tale and the inspiration for Hardin Wolton. You taught me that with hard work anything is possible. Thank you.

To my kids, Theo and Raina. Being your mom is the best gift I could ever ask for. Always pursue your dreams!

To my husband, Bart, my Bear and the love of my life. You always unfailingly believe in me. I love you so much.

And lastly, to Sarah Williams, CEO of Serenade

Publishing for believing in what I have written and giving me the opportunity to share it with others. I am forever grateful.

9 780645 713367